CASTRATION CELEBRATION

ALSO BY JAKE WIZNER

Spanking Shakespeare

CASTRATION CELEBRATION

JAKE WIZNER

RANDOM HOUSE NEW YORK

Text copyright © 2009 by Jake Wizner
Jacket photographs 1, 2 © Brand X Pictures/Royalty-Free Jupiterimages;
photographs 3, 5, 6 © Mike Kemp/Rubberball/Jupiterimages;
photograph 4 © Erik Isakson/Rubberball/Jupiterimages

Visit us on the Web! www.randomhouse.com/teens

Educators and librarians, for a variety of teaching tools,
visit us at www.randomhouse.com/teachers

Library of Congress Cataloging-in-Publication Data
Wizner, Jake.
Castration Celebration / Jake Wizner. — 1st ed.
p.   cm.
Summary: Three high school students in a summer arts program at Yale University
collaborate on an "anti-guy musical" with the working title, Castration Celebration.
ISBN 978-0-375-85215-2 (trade) — ISBN 978-0-375-95215-9 (lib. bdg.) —
ISBN 978-0-375-85216-9 (trade pbk.) — ISBN 978-0-375-85217-6 (mass-market pbk.)
ISBN 978-0-375-85391-3 (e-book)
[1. Interpersonal relations—Fiction. 2. Authorship—Fiction. 3. Musicals—Fiction.
4. Family problems—Fiction. 5. Drug abuse—Fiction. 6. Universities and
colleges—Fiction. 7. New Haven (Conn.)—Fiction.] I. Title.
PZ7.W791Cas 2009
[Fic]—dc22
2008026695

Printed in the United States of America
10 9 8 7 6 5 4 3 2 1
First Edition

For **KIRA, LEILANI,** and **CECILY**

PROLOGUE

Olivia was sitting on top of her new suitcase in the courtyard of Yale's Old Campus writing in her notebook. She had scrawled the word *CASTRATION* on the top of the page and was in the process of listing genital-based rhymes. So far her list read: *menstruation, masturbation, elongation, lubrication, penetration, stimulation, fornication, copulation, urination, ejaculation, insemination.* She had always had a perverse sense of humor, and it had become even more twisted over the past year as any illusions she had clung to of a happy family had been blown away. "Blown" was of course the operative word, as in, *I walked into my father's office and saw him being blown by one of his graduate students.* Such a lovely picture. One to file away to entertain the kids on a rainy day if the Ritalin jar was empty. She leaned back over her notebook and started a new column. *Extermination, emasculation, suffocation, asphyxiation . . .*

Max was walking across the campus courtyard talking on his cell phone and paying scant attention to the world around him.

His side of the conversation sounded like this: "I'm telling you, Andy, she was twenty-one and totally smoking. . . . Dude, we were on a crowded train, how am I supposed to make out with her? I got her phone number, though. . . . I don't know. I mean, I'm about to spend the whole summer living in a coed dorm. And besides, she wasn't very smart. She actually believed I was a sophomore at Yale. . . . Dude, the only reason you like stupid chicks is because any girl with half a brain won't go out with you. I'm ready for someone who has some substance, you know, someone with an edge. . . ."

BANG!

Max's shin hit Olivia's suitcase, and he toppled forward onto Olivia, who was facing away from him. She pitched forward, he bounced off her back, she dropped her notebook, he dropped his cell phone, and they both cried out in surprise.

"Jesus," Olivia said, looking at a sprawled-out Max. "What the hell?"

Max pushed himself up. "I'm so sorry. I didn't even see you there."

Olivia picked up her notebook, stood, and brushed herself off.

"Are you okay?" he asked.

She nodded.

"You sure?"

Olivia looked the boy over. He had that cultivated scruffy look she might have found appealing if he had not just body-slammed her, and if she had not sworn off boys for the more satisfying pursuit of filling up notebooks with rants about infidelity, castration, and patricide. "Yeah," she said, offering a quick smile.

"I was just thinking it's been a while since I've had any good spinal damage."

She was surprisingly attractive, Max realized, in the way smart girls with a sense of humor, red hair, and good skin can be. "How are your kidneys?" he asked.

"Fine," she said. "Ready to excrete."

He laughed and held out his hand. "I'm Max."

She paused a moment before shaking it. "Olivia."

"Are you here for the summer arts program?"

"Yeah," she said, pulling the program ID, attached to a looped blue ribbon, out of her pocket. "I guess I'm supposed to wear this."

"Is that so they can keep tabs on us?" Max asked.

Olivia shrugged. "At least we don't have to wear electronic ankle bracelets."

"Right," Max said, "because I'm sure a program like this draws some pretty unsavory characters." He looked over at the registration line across the courtyard and then turned back to Olivia. "So what are you here for?"

She paused a moment and then said, "Assault with a deadly weapon."

"Really," Max said, laughing. "Who's the victim?"

Olivia was unable to suppress a grin. "Believe me, you're better off not knowing."

"Why's that?"

She unzipped her book bag and slid her notebook inside. "Trust me on this one."

"I'm intrigued," he said.

She smiled at him. It was nice to know she could intrigue

Demolition Derby Boy so easily. "I'm just trying to protect you," she said, zipping her bag quickly and getting a little piece of canvas stuck under the teeth of the zipper. "It's sensitive stuff we're dealing with here." She yanked hard, and the zipper came free.

"I think I can handle it," Max said.

"I'm sure you can," she chuckled. Grabbing her suitcase, she gave Max a long look and then said, "Sorry to cut and run, but I'm going to head up to my room now."

"Well," he said with a grin, "it was nice bumping into you."

She rolled her eyes, turned, and walked away.

CHAPTER ONE

Olivia entered her suite to find a Barbie look-alike already there, listening to her iPod and dancing around the common room in impossibly short shorts and a midriff-baring T-shirt. When she spotted Olivia, she smiled hugely and pulled off her headphones. "Oh my God!" she squealed. "I know you. You were right in front of me in line before!"

"Small world," Olivia said with a smirk.

"I'm Mimi," Barbie said. "We're the only ones here so far. You want to share a room with me?" She pointed to the bedroom on the left. "It's a little bigger, I think."

Oh God, Olivia thought. She looked toward the bedroom, but did not move.

"Plus it's got better feng shooey, because the beds are farther from the door."

Feng shooey? Olivia stifled a laugh. Just for the raw material Mimi would provide, maybe it would be worth it to share. And there really was no graceful way to turn down the offer without hurting Mimi's feelings. "How can I say no to better feng shooey?" Olivia said, beginning to wheel her suitcase to the left.

Mimi followed her into the room. "How funny is it that we're roommates and we checked in at exactly the same time? I mean, check-in is all day, so we could have come at any time. It's like fate, or something, that we ended up roommates, don't you think?"

Keep a straight face, Olivia told herself, and don't say anything too sarcastic. She placed her suitcase flat next to her bed and began to unzip it. Maybe if she didn't respond, Mimi would stop talking.

"I mean what are the chances that we'd be right next to each other at registration? Like a million to one, right?"

"Yeah, it's a good thing I stopped to get drunk on the way here this morning," Olivia blurted, "or we would have totally missed each other."

"Are you serious?" Mimi's eyes popped wide. "No, you're kidding."

"I probably shouldn't drink when I'm on so many painkillers, but, hey, it's summer, right?"

Mimi's expression veered from amusement to serious concern, and Olivia burst out laughing.

"Oh my God!" Mimi squealed. "I totally believed you for a second!"

Olivia shook her head. "Don't worry, I'm actually a pretty straight arrow. No drinking, no drugs, nothing illegal for me."

"Well, that's a relief." Mimi plopped down on her bed and her voice took on a playful quality. "What about boys?"

"Definitely none of them," Olivia said decisively.

"Get out!" Mimi shrieked. "Have you seen all the hot guys here?"

Olivia chuckled. Just her luck to get stuck with a nympho-maniac.

In the same dorm, one floor below, Max was unpacking when a tall, skinny guy with long hair walked into the room, wheeling a huge suitcase, wearing a backpack over one shoulder, and carrying a guitar.

"Hey," Max said.

The guy gave a little nod. "What's up?"

"I'm Max."

"Zeke." He dropped the backpack on the empty bed and leaned his guitar against the wall.

"You here for music?" Max asked.

"Yeah."

Zeke opened his book bag, fished out a bottle of water, and took a big swig. Then he brushed his hair out of his face and lifted his suitcase onto the bed.

"You'd think with how much money we're paying we'd get a bigger room, right?" Max said.

"At least some air-conditioning."

"I know. This room's like a fucking sauna."

"You think any of the rooms have air-conditioning?" Zeke asked.

"If they do, I'm requesting a transfer. No offense."

Max was actually feeling pretty happy about his roommate situation. For all he knew, he might have ended up with a violin prodigy named Vladimir, who practiced eight hours a day and was several years away from either Carnegie Hall or a complete nervous breakdown. Zeke, on the other hand, seemed like the kind of guy who would be up for almost anything. A young Joey Ramone.

"So," Max said, pointing to Zeke's guitar. "What kind of music do you play?"

Zeke brushed his hair back with his hands. "I don't know. Mostly my own stuff, I guess."

"You in a band?"

Zeke shook his head. "Used to be."

"What happened?"

Zeke shrugged. "Lead singer kind of dropped out. Band just fell apart after that."

Max put on his best TV voice. "They had everything going for them: a hit album, a sold-out concert tour, and a multi-record deal, but behind the scenes, trouble was brewing in paradise. In-fighting and drug abuse were threatening to pull the band apart, and when lead singer . . ." He reverted to his own voice. "What was your lead singer's name?"

Zeke hesitated. "Devin Baines," he said.

"And when lead singer Devin Baines overdosed on painkillers just before a sold-out show at Madison Square Garden, it looked like the band's days were numbered."

"You watch too much VH1," Zeke said, turning away.

"Probably," Max agreed.

Zeke unzipped his suitcase, took out an iPod dock, and put it on the shelf of his desk. "You can use this," he said, plugging it in, "but no Celine Dion when I'm in the room."

Upstairs in Olivia and Mimi's suite, the two remaining girls—Trish and Callie—had arrived, and the foursome was complete. At the moment, they were sitting two and two on the couches in the common room, and Mimi was gushing over Callie's short, spiky hair and the multiple studs in each ear.

"It's like so punk rock, you know. Do boys like that?"

Callie seemed mildly amused. "I wouldn't know. I've never asked them."

"Do you think I'd look good with short hair?" Mimi pulled her hair up and bunched it against the back of her head.

"With your body, you'd look good bald," Trish said, folding her arms across her stomach.

"Shut up," Mimi said delightedly. She jumped up and bounded into the bedroom to look in a mirror. A few seconds passed, and then she called, "What's everyone wearing to dinner tonight?"

Olivia threw a knowing smile at Trish and Callie. "Pretty spectacular, isn't she?"

Callie rolled her eyes.

"I wasn't planning to change," Trish said, as Mimi walked back into the room.

Olivia feigned shock. "You're going to wear jeans and an oversize Yale T-shirt? With all the cute boys here?"

Trish shrugged. "Why, what are you wearing?"

Olivia thought for a moment. "I was thinking about a miniskirt, fishnets, and"—she snapped her fingers—"some white cowboy boots."

Callie nodded. "Now that's fierce."

"With a dark green halter to go with your red hair," Mimi said. "Oh my God, that would be adorable."

Trish shook her head. "With your body you can get away with it. I need clothes that cover as much of my fat as possible."

"You are so not fat," Mimi said.

"Well, I doubt any boys are going to be looking at me anyway if I'm sitting with the three of you."

"Oh my God, that's so not true," Mimi said. She turned to the other girls. "Don't you think Trish is like so pretty? Look at that perfect button nose."

"Plus you've got the biggest boobs," Callie said.

Trish laughed.

"And I'm not interested in boys, anyway," Olivia said.

Callie turned and stared hard at her.

"She's crazy," Mimi said.

"Actually, I'm not into them, either," Callie said. She smiled at Olivia, and Olivia smiled back.

"I am," Trish said. "They're just not into me."

"Wait," Mimi said, turning to Callie. "You don't like boys, either?" She looked genuinely perplexed. "Why not?"

Olivia giggled. This was going to be good.

"I like girls," Callie said matter-of-factly.

Mimi's eyes popped wide. "You're gay?"

"Do you have a problem with that?"

"Why would we have a problem with it?" Olivia said.

"Oh my God," Mimi said, turning to Olivia. "Are you gay, too?"

Olivia laughed and shook her head. "No. I just have some penis issues to work out."

"It was unbelievable," Max said. "I mean, after I crashed into her, our eyes just locked, and my skin started to tingle, and it was like we had this connection. Like we were totally locked into each other and everything around us just melted away, you know?"

Zeke picked up his guitar and unzipped the case.

"It was weird, man. I mean, she's good-looking and all, but it wasn't her looks, it was more the *way* she looked *at* me. Like she was sizing me up or something. That's the way the whole thing felt when we were talking, too. Like she knew something I didn't know and was daring me to guess."

"Huh," Zeke said, beginning to tune his guitar.

Max plunged on, barely registering Zeke's lack of interest. "I mean, I've gone out with girls who were prettier than her, but no one who was that quick. You know what she said? When I asked her why she was here, you know like for acting or music, she said she was here for assault with a deadly weapon. That's funny, right?"

"Hilarious."

"I'm telling you," Max said. "Just talking to her was a totally exhilarating experience. She's just got this edge, you know. I like girls who are edgy."

Zeke strummed a few chords and looked up. "I like girls who are naked."

Max smiled. "That's what I'm talking about."

"You're writing a musical about castration?" Trish said in disbelief. "That's hysterical."

Callie nodded approvingly. "It's long overdue."

"Hello, am I like in *The Twilight Zone* or something?" Mimi asked, looking up from the floor where she was applying a fresh coat of red nail polish to her toenails. "Why does everyone here hate penises so much?"

"Technically, it's not the penis I'm cutting off. It's the testicles."

"Really?" Trish said. "I always thought castration meant cutting off the penis."

"You know," Callie said, "in Imperial China, to become a eunuch, you had to have your testicles, penis, *and* scrotum removed."

Mimi scrunched up her face. "Ewww."

"And then the eunuch would preserve them in alcohol so they could be buried with him when he died, and he would be reborn with all his parts intact."

"I don't get it," Mimi said. "If he wants it all back, why cut it off in the first place?"

"You know what would be cool?" Olivia said. "You know how toy stores have doctor kits for kids to play with? What if they sold miniature castration kits?"

Callie laughed. "I mutilated most of my dolls anyway."

"There you go," Olivia continued. "And it could come with detachable genitalia, and a little jar to store the testicles in."

"And a knife to do the cutting," Callie added.

"Can we please talk about something else?" Mimi pleaded.

"It's a great idea," Trish said. "You could mass-produce them in China, since it's kind of their thing anyway. Except you'd probably get lead in the balls."

"You know," Olivia said, "you could actually put out a whole series of genital-related toys." Her cell phone rang in the bed-room and she jumped up. "Like how about the do-it-yourself circumcision kit?" she said, hurrying into the other room.

Grabbing her phone, she looked at the caller ID and sighed. Why were they calling already? The whole point of going away for the summer was to be away. She'd have to establish some ground rules.

"Hi, Mom," she said. "I can't really talk right now. . . ." She hovered in the doorway. "Everything's good. Tell Lucy I'll call her." She hung up just in time to hear Trish say, "Bikini-waxing Barbie, with detachable pubic hair."

Olivia clapped as she returned to the couch. "Brilliant. A few more, and we can go into business."

"Menstruating Mandy," Callie said. "Wind her up and watch her squirt."

"Ewww," Mimi said as the other girls burst into laughter.

"What time is dinner?" Max asked. "I'm starving."

"I don't know. Six, I think."

"Man, I've hardly eaten anything all day. You didn't bring any food, did you?"

Zeke dug his hand into his pocket. "I think I've got some Tic Tacs."

"I'll take anything."

Zeke was still digging. "I thought I had some." He unzipped an outside pocket of his book bag and pulled out the contents.

"Are those rolling papers?" Max asked, reaching out and picking up a small flat cardboard package.

"Oh, yeah," Zeke said as noncommittally as possible.

"Did you bring any dope?" Max asked excitedly.

Zeke looked up and smiled. "You like to smoke?"

"Hell, yeah. Did you bring anything?"

Zeke shrugged. "I might have a little something."

"Sweet," Max said. "Let me see?"

Zeke unzipped an inside pocket of his book bag, pulled out a baggie, and handed it to Max.

"Jesus," Max said, his eyes popping wide. "How much is this?"

"About half an ounce."

Max stared at the contents of the bag in amazement. It was more than he had ever bought himself, and it looked fresher, greener than anything he could remember seeing back home in New Orleans. He opened the bag and sniffed. "Whoa," he said. "That is some stinky weed."

"You want to roll a joint?"

"Now?" Max shook his head and handed back the baggie. "I don't think so. I want to be coherent at dinner, especially if I see Olivia."

"Yeah, this stuff will fuck you up pretty bad."

"I can't believe you brought half an ounce of pot," Max said. "We should definitely smoke some of that later."

Zeke nodded and put the baggie back in his book bag. "We should pick up some munchy food. Some Pringles, you know?"

"Definitely," Max said. "And maybe a couple of pizzas, too."

"I've got a boy I bet you'll like," Olivia said. She was sitting on her bed watching Mimi put on pink lipstick in preparation for dinner. "I met him just before I came up to the room."

"Is he cute? What's his name?"

"Max." Or better yet, Mad Max, she thought, remembering the way he had barreled into her. "He kind of looks like Jake Gyllenhaal."

"Oh my God, I love Jake Gyllenhaal!" Mimi screeched, turning away from the mirror. "Let's sit with him at dinner."

Olivia laughed. "Feeling hungry, are we?"

"Ewww," Mimi said, grabbing a pillow and hitting Olivia playfully. Olivia grabbed a pillow and hit Mimi back.

"What are you two doing in here?" Callie said, appearing in the doorway.

"Having an orgy," Olivia said. "You want to join us?"

"Olivia!" Mimi sounded scandalized.

"Don't worry," Callie said. "Neither of you is my type, anyway. Come on, dinner starts in five minutes."

The girls dropped their pillows back on their beds and headed out, joining the clusters of other summer students streaming toward the dining hall in search of sustenance, a human mass pulsing with all the excitement and nervousness and possibility of a brand-new beginning in a brand-new world.

CHAPTER TWO

Max saw Olivia and three other girls settling in at a table across the dining hall and motioned for Zeke to follow him. As they approached, Trish looked up and a smile broke over her face.

"Hey, Zeke," she said. "Come sit with us. This is my friend, Zeke," she told the other girls as the boys sat down. "We go to school together in Saratoga."

Max smiled at Olivia first and then at the others, his eyes lingering a moment on Mimi, who was wearing a low-cut shirt that might as well have said "Boy Magnet" across the front. "I'm Max," he said.

"Hey, Max," Olivia said, elbowing Mimi gently. "These are my roommates Mimi, Trish, and Callie."

"Hi," Mimi said. She leaned toward Olivia and whispered, "He's so hot," before turning back and eating him up with her eyes.

"So you guys are friends from school?" Olivia asked, looking from Trish to Heavy Metal Rocker Boy, and thinking that they were about as unlikely a pair as she could imagine.

Trish nodded. "We actually wrote a musical together this year for our English class. Zeke's an amazing musician." She smiled at Zeke, and he looked down at his tray.

"You write music?" Olivia asked him.

Zeke nodded. "Sometimes."

"I was the one who convinced Zeke to come this summer," Trish said, flashing him another smile. "Aren't you so glad I did?"

"Ecstatic," Zeke said, taking a bite of mashed potatoes.

"Well, *I'm* glad," Max said. He looked again at Olivia and noticed that she had changed into a green T-shirt and that her red hair was hanging loose and that her skin was even creamier than he remembered. "So, all recovered from this afternoon?" he asked her.

"Physically or emotionally?"

He smiled, and she smiled back.

"Why, what happened?" Mimi asked.

"I kind of ran over her." He recapped the story, using the salt and pepper shakers on the table to provide a visual of the collision and enhancing the account with exaggerated sound effects.

"He basically crushed me," Olivia said.

Mimi looked at Max. "Sounds fun."

He smiled again at Olivia. "I like to leave a lasting impression."

All around them the dining room was coming to life, and the sounds of talking and laughter and chairs scraping against the floor echoed through the room. Most of the tables were segregated by gender, the students choosing the security of their same-sex hallmates on this first night. But for Max, talking to girls had always been easy, and he felt a tinge of self-satisfaction being surrounded now, not just by four girls, but by four good-looking girls. He began to scrutinize them as he ate, trying to rank them in the order that he would like to sleep with them.

Olivia was trying hard not to think about how cute Max was. He was a flirt, and the kind of boy who would try to hook up with as many girls as possible over the next six weeks. In that way, he and Mimi were flip sides of the same coin, and she should just sit back and let the inevitable coupling run its course. But there was no reason why she shouldn't have the fun of bantering with him. He was sharp, and she liked the challenge of trading barbs. Now, seeing him sizing up her roommates, she pounced.

"You look like a boy in a candy store, Max."

He blushed at having been caught, but recovered quickly. "I can think of worse places to be."

"So many sweets to choose from, aren't there?" she said, smiling mischievously.

"It's true," he said, glancing around the dining hall. "How do you pick just one?"

"Maybe you don't."

He looked at her and nodded. Here was the spark he had felt before, and he plunged ahead with abandon. "So you think it's okay to splurge?"

"I wouldn't know. I don't eat candy." She popped a piece of cucumber into her mouth.

Callie laughed, and Max turned to her.

"Don't waste your time," Olivia said. "You're not her flavor."

Max looked momentarily confused, and all the girls started to laugh.

"She likes girls," Mimi said helpfully.

"Ohhh, I get it." He smiled at Callie and said, "We have a lot in common."

She shook her head, grinned, and cut a bite of chicken.

He pointed at his plate. "Look, we both chose breasts."

"Oh God," Olivia said as Trish and Mimi began to laugh.

He turned back to Olivia. "So you don't eat *any* candy?"

She shook her head. "Just gum. I like to chew it up and spit it out."

"Nice one," Callie said appreciatively.

Max held Olivia's gaze. "No sucking or swallowing, huh?"

"Jesus," Zeke said, dropping his fork on his tray. The girls, including Olivia, laughed.

"Can you blow big bubbles?" Max persisted.

Olivia impaled a cherry tomato. "I can pop big egos."

"Touché," Trish said, and reached over to give Olivia a high five.

"Hey, enough being mean," Mimi said.

"It's okay," Max said. "We're just playing."

"Well, how about something we can all play together. Like let's go around and everybody say your favorite kind of candy for real."

"Definitely Pixy Stix," Trish said. "Remember those? You'd break them open and suck out the sugar inside?"

"Wow, I haven't seen those in forever," Callie said.

"We have this place near us." Trish turned to Zeke. "You know Tuffy's Sweet Shop? Anyway, they've got like every kind of candy imaginable. I used to go there every day after school and buy like six packs of Pixy Stix." She smiled fondly in recollection. "I guess

19

that's why I'm about thirty pounds heavier than anyone else at this table."

"Shut up," Mimi said, "you so are not."

"I like Cadbury Creme Eggs," Callie said. "They remind me of a vagina."

"Ewww, gross," Mimi said as the rest of the table burst out laughing.

"What about you, Mimi?" Max asked. "What's your favorite?"

"I don't know," she said. "There are so many. Maybe Nerds."

Olivia smiled. "You like Nerds, Mimi?"

"Oh my God, I love them."

"How many can you put in your mouth at once?" Callie asked, and everyone started to laugh again.

"Ewww," Mimi said, blushing. "You guys are like so perverted."

"How about you, Zeke?" Trish asked. "What kind of candy do you like?"

He shrugged. "I don't know. Sour Patch Kids are pretty good."

"Figures," Trish said. She turned to the others. "Zeke's not much of a talker. We drove here together, and he barely said two words the whole way."

"I think it's refreshing to meet a boy who doesn't feel the need to hear his own voice all the time," Olivia said.

"Oh, are we going another round?" Max asked.

"I'm ready."

"Please, no," Zeke said. "It's exhausting just listening to you two."

Olivia laughed. "Okay, I'll shut up now."

"I like Sour Patch Kids, too," Max said to Zeke. He shifted his gaze and looked meaningfully at Olivia. "I like things that are tart on the outside, but sweet underneath."

She shook her head, amused. "Who said anything about being sweet?"

A little later, after the group had exchanged opinions about the food (it tasted like fecal matter), the dorms (way too hot), and the eleven o'clock curfew (total bullshit), conversation turned to where everyone was from and how they had ended up at Yale for the summer. When Max announced that he had come to take acting classes, Mimi nearly leapt from her seat in excitement.

"Oh my God," she said, reaching out and touching his arm. "Me too. We could be partners when we do acting exercises. Do you know the mirror game?"

"Everyone knows the mirror game, Mimi," Callie said.

Max took a sip of apple juice. "I had an acting teacher once who used to make us stand in a circle, and then she'd call out a body part and we'd have to communicate what we wanted just using that one part of the body."

"Oh my God, we should totally play right now," Mimi said.

Olivia shook her head. "No, thanks. You actors are a bit too wild and crazy for me."

"Me too," Zeke said, standing and picking up his tray. "I'll see you all later."

Trish frowned. "You're going? What are you up to tonight?"

"I don't know. Just heading back to the dorm."

"Hey," Max said. "You want me to get . . . ?" He gave Zeke a knowing look.

Zeke shook his head. "I'm on it."

What to do after dinner became the focus of conversation. Trish suggested an ice cream place she knew about near campus, and after a loving description of the bittersweet dark chocolate—*the best thing you've ever eaten*—Mimi and Callie signed on.

"You guys are coming, too, right?" Mimi asked Olivia and Max.

"I'm going to pass," Olivia said, standing and picking up her tray. "I'll see you guys back at the dorm."

"I'll go with you," Max said, jumping up. "I should finish unpacking."

"You're not coming?" Mimi said, giving Max a pouty look. "Come on. You can unpack later."

Max looked from Mimi to Olivia.

"Go ahead," Olivia said. "I can walk back by myself."

Max hesitated a moment, and then looked purposefully at his watch. "I need to head back. I've got some stuff I have to finish." He turned to Olivia and raised his eyebrows.

She looked at Mimi and shrugged. "See you guys later, I guess," she said, and marched off to bus her tray, with Max trailing behind.

They exited the dining hall and followed a small group of summer students back out onto York Street.

"You don't mind that I left with you, do you?" Max asked.

She turned to him. "No, why?"

"I don't know," he said, looking straight ahead. "It kind of seemed like you wanted me to go with them."

She laughed. "I think that's what Mimi wanted."

He nodded and grinned. "You think?"

"Oh, yeah. I'm sure she would have *loved* to share something sweet with you."

They turned right off York onto Elm Street. "That's not really the taste I'm in the mood for," Max said.

Olivia grimaced and quickly recovered without Max noticing. She continued to walk forward without talking, and without responding to what Max had said.

"Have you been here before?" he asked.

"To New Haven?"

He nodded.

"Yeah. I live in Hartford."

"Insurance capital of America," Max said.

They arrived back at the Old Campus and walked into the courtyard and toward the dorm.

"So," Max said, "what are you up to now?"

Olivia shrugged. "Getting ready to start classes tomorrow, you know."

"You want to go sit on the stairs over there for a little?" He pointed across the courtyard.

"I don't know," she said. "I think I might just head in."

"Come on," he said, taking her hand. "It's so nice out."

She gently detached her hand from his.

"Sorry," he said.

She stopped, and they stood there looking at each other. "Listen," she said. "I'm sorry if I gave you the wrong idea at dinner."

Max forced a smile. "It's okay. I wasn't making a pass at you or anything."

She gave him a skeptical look. "You weren't?"

He shrugged. "Well, maybe I was a little bit."

She shook her head. "We just met, Max."

"Haven't you ever heard of love at first sight?" he said half-jokingly.

"Oh, Jesus." She started walking again toward the dorm.

"You have a boyfriend, don't you?" Max said, hurrying to catch up.

She shook her head. "No."

"So what is it then?"

"I'm here to work this summer," she said, without breaking stride.

"So am I. It doesn't mean we can't have fun."

"We don't even know each other. You don't know anything about me."

"I know you don't have a boyfriend," he said. "And I assume you're not a lesbian."

She smiled, despite herself. "It's not going to happen, Max."

"Why not?"

"It's just not." They were right outside the dorm now and she stopped and faced him. "Look, I'm sure there are plenty of girls here who would be happy to go out with you. Mimi was practically drooling on you at dinner."

"Drooling? Wow. Come on, Olivia, do you think I'm interested in a girl who can't hold on to her own saliva?"

"Aren't you?"

"No." He reached out and took her hand again. "At least not Mimi's saliva," he said more softly.

She looked at him for a second, and then gently pulled her hand away. "I'm going to go in now," she said.

She turned her back and walked quickly inside, leaving Max to wonder how something that had seemed so right had suddenly gone so wrong.

CHAPTER THREE

Zeke had dimmed the lights in the room, stuffed a towel under the door, and put Pink Floyd's *Dark Side of the Moon* on the iPod. The joint he had rolled was a masterpiece—tightly packed, perfectly cylindrical, and burning strong as he and Max passed it back and forth. When Zeke held the joint, it conformed to his hand like a sixth finger, and when he put it to his mouth, he inhaled long and deep, never coughing, just cradling the smoke in his mouth and lungs and then releasing it into the air in a majestic burst.

Max felt the room starting to spin, and so when Zeke held out the joint to him yet again, he just shook his head.

"You pretty baked?" Zeke asked.

"Oh my God, I'm fried out of my mind."

Zeke smiled, took another hit, and stubbed out the joint. "Told you this shit was good."

"It's like Superweed," Max said, stretching out on his bed but using his pillow to keep his head propped up. "More powerful than a bird, stronger than a plane, it's a bird, it's a plane, it's Superweed."

"What the fuck are you talking about?" Zeke said, laughing.

"Holy shit, I can't even talk straight."

Zeke took a sip of water and smiled. "Good thing you're a lightweight. I need this shit to last me all summer."

"I think you have enough," Max said.

"I've got a friend back home who would smoke this in a week."

"Are you serious?" Max said, laughing. "No way."

"I've seen him do it." Zeke reached for his water bottle and took a long drink.

Max lifted his hand in front of his face and stared at it intently. "Have you ever really looked at your hand before? It's pretty wild."

"Try saying the alphabet backward," Zeke said.

Max dropped his hand and made a serious effort to focus. "Z, Y, X." He paused for a second to run through the letters in his head. "W, U, V . . . Fuck, I can't deal with that right now."

"Check this out," Zeke said. And without warning he rattled off the backward alphabet at lightning speed.

"Whoa," Max said, looking thoroughly spooked. "Dude, don't ever do that again when I'm high."

Zeke laughed. "That's fucked up, right?"

"I think I need to lie down." Max placed his pillow flat on the bed and sank down on his back. He couldn't remember the last time he had been so high, and this, combined with the strangeness of the whole day, was making him feel thoroughly disoriented. If he could just sleep now, he would wake up with a clear head and be able to start fresh. He tried closing his eyes, and as he did, his cell phone rang, and he sat up with a jolt and looked at the caller ID. "Oh, shit," he said.

"Who is it?"

Max shook his head and flipped open his phone. "Hey, Dad. . . . Yeah. All good, all good, you know. . . ." He held the cell phone away from him and made funny faces at it, cracking Zeke up. "Hey, Dad," he said, putting the phone back to his ear, "we've got some people over, you know, so I should run. I'll call you tomorrow. . . . Yeah. Bye. Bye. Bye." He closed the phone and flopped back on his bed.

"You're a freak," Zeke said.

"Did I sound totally fried?"

"Not at all. Why did you even answer, though?"

Max sat up and leaned against the wall. "I told my dad I'd call, and I forgot. I didn't want him freaking out and calling the program director or police or something."

"Are you serious?"

"Who knows? I wouldn't put it past him."

"What's his deal?" Zeke asked.

Max shrugged. "It's just him and me, so he's always been all overprotective and shit."

"What happened to your mom?" Zeke asked.

Max held his hand in front of his face again and began to wriggle his fingers. "She left when I was five."

Zeke watched for a moment without speaking. "That sucks, man," he finally said, getting up and pulling a bag of Nacho Cheese Doritos from a shopping bag on the floor. He opened it and held it out to Max. "They didn't have any Pringles."

"Fuck Pringles," Max said, reaching out and taking a handful of chips. "I like these better."

Zeke popped a chip in his mouth and crunched. "So do you ever see her?"

Max shook his head. "We never really knew where she was. My dad says she called a few times, but never from a number we could call her back."

"That's rough."

Max nodded and chewed on a chip. "She was hot, though."

"Jesus," Zeke said, grimacing. "That's your mom."

Max laughed and savored the nacho cheese goodness in his mouth. It was amazing how delicious things could taste when you were high. He thought about the fact that this morning he had woken up in his bed in New Orleans, and now here he was sitting in a college dorm room at Yale, fried out of his mind, eating Nacho Cheese Doritos. It was crazy.

"We're at fucking Yale University," he said.

Zeke smiled. "You sound like Trish. She's totally obsessed with this place."

"Oh, yeah, what's the deal with you guys anyway?"

"What do you mean?"

Max reached out and took the bag of chips. "Did you guys ever go out or anything?"

Zeke screwed up his face. "No."

"Why not?"

"Would you go out with her?"

Max tried to picture her in his head. She had been a little overweight, maybe, but not bad. "I don't know," he said. "She's got big tits."

"Well, if you're interested, go for it."

He remembered with a pang what had happened with Olivia.

"Let me ask you something," he said. "At dinner, didn't you think Olivia was kind of flirting with me?"

Zeke ate his last chip. "I don't know."

"Seriously," Max said. "Didn't it seem like we had a connection?"

"Yeah, you were both annoying," Zeke said, getting up to change the music.

Max smiled and gave Zeke the finger. "It was weird. After dinner, when I tried to talk to her, she totally blew me off."

Zeke scrolled through his iPod until he found *Blood on the Tracks*. "Whatever, man. There are plenty of girls here."

"What do you think her problem is?" Max asked.

The opening strains of "Tangled Up in Blue" came on and Zeke stood by the desk, gently bobbing his head to the music.

"Well," Max said. "What do you think?"

"It's the first night," Zeke said, sitting back on his bed. "What did you think would happen?"

"I don't know."

They sat listening to the music, but Max's head was filled with Olivia, how he had taken her hand, and how she had pulled away and walked off. Had he really only met her this afternoon? What had he been thinking making a pass at her so soon?

"You know what I think?" Zeke said, as if reading his thoughts.

"What?"

"I think we should smoke the rest of that joint."

Max laughed. "Are you trying to kill me?"

"Dude, it's summer vacation. You're at Yale. And sitting in that shopping bag on the floor, waiting to be eaten, is an entire bag of Funyuns."

"You're out of control."

"Funyuns, Max. Do you understand?"

Max nodded slowly, like someone in a trance. "I do. I do understand."

Zeke took the joint from the windowsill, relit it, took a drag, and held it out to his roommate.

"Unbelievable," Max said, shaking his head and taking a hit. He blew out the smoke and looked at Zeke. "I'm going to get Olivia to go out with me, you know."

Zeke reached for the joint and inhaled deeply.

"I mean, it's only the first night, right? We've got the whole summer ahead of us."

Zeke passed the joint back to Max and blew out a tremendous cloud of smoke.

"Jesus," Max said with admiration, "you're like a professional pot smoker or something."

"Stronger than a bird," Zeke said.

"Stronger than a fucking plane," Max said, laughing. He took a hit and dissolved into a fit of uncontrollable coughing.

CHAPTER FOUR

Olivia's playwriting teacher, Maxine Zbotsky, had experienced her fifteen minutes of fame three decades earlier for her inflammatory musical, *I Came, I Came, I Came Again.* Since that time, she had married and divorced twice, become a devotee of several Eastern religions, dabbled with astrology, temporarily changed her name to Artemis Moon Goddess, lived on a commune in Northern California, hiked the Appalachian Trail, bungee jumped in Australia, and purchased 187 Elvis figurines on eBay.

Olivia did not know any of this. All she knew was that her teacher was already seven minutes late to class on the first day and people were starting to get antsy.

"What kind of teacher shows up late the first day?" she asked Trish, who was sitting next to her in the U-shaped arrangement of desks.

"It's a summer program," Trish said. "Everything's probably looser and more laid-back than at school."

"The amount of money they're charging, you'd think they'd hire teachers who show up on time," said a boy on the other side of Trish.

There were only ten students in the class, and all around people nodded in agreement.

"I hear she's a total freak," a mousy-looking girl chimed in.

"Now what would give you that idea?" said an amused voice. Resplendent in a silky wrap of purple, bracelets jangling on her wrists, graying hair in two long braids, silver sandals on her feet, Maxine glided from the doorway into the room. The students in the class smiled, laughed, and sat transfixed, and the mousy-looking girl tried to disappear into her chair.

"Lesson number one," she said, her eyes moving from face to face. "You've only got one chance to make a first impression, so make sure you start with a bang." She clapped her hands together loudly. "Now open your notebooks and let's begin."

Olivia rushed to comply, charged by her teacher's dramatic entrance. All around her students were opening notebooks and sitting expectantly, pens poised, eyes fixed on the purple-clad woman up front.

"Okay," Maxine said. "I want each of you to think about something really disturbing, and then write down whatever it is. Two minutes. Go."

People seemed slightly stunned, and a few hands rose tentatively in the air.

"No questions," Maxine said. "Just write whatever comes to mind."

Some students, including Trish, were already going. Others

sat with troubled expressions, trying to figure out what to put down. After a moment, Olivia began to write, though with a lack of conviction.

Men are in charge of everything in this world. That's why we're so screwed.

She had just finished writing when Maxine called time and asked for volunteers to share. People looked around uncomfortably, but nobody raised a hand.

"Nobody?" Maxine said, surprised. "Wow, you must all have some really disturbing thoughts."

The boy sitting next to Trish raised his hand. He struck Olivia as the kind of boy who liked to talk a lot in class but probably didn't put much thought into what he said. Maybe it was the fact that he had broad shoulders and almost no neck.

"Fabulous, a volunteer." Maxine clapped her hands. "Your name?"

"Bruce Ackerman," the boy said.

Bruce. How perfect.

"Okay, Bruce Ackerman, shock and disturb us."

Bruce looked down at his notebook and started to read. "More people vote for the American Idol than for the American president."

A few people chuckled. Olivia decided that maybe he wasn't quite as much of an idiot as she had thought.

"Well, that certainly is disturbing," Maxine said. "Thank you for sharing. Anyone else?"

Trish raised her hand.

"Your name, dear?" Maxine asked.

"Trish Aiken."

"Okay, Trish Aiken, the stage is yours."

"In Imperial China, to be a eunuch, you had to remove your penis, testicles, and scrotum, and then preserve them in a jar of alcohol to be buried with you when you died."

There were a few exclamations of disgust, and several boys moved their hands protectively over their laps. Olivia laughed and whispered, "Cheater."

"I don't think the boys liked that one much," Maxine said with a chuckle. She looked for other hands and, when there were none forthcoming, said, "Okay, let's try this one more time, but change the rules a little bit. This time, whatever you write has to be about you in some way."

Shocked looks and nervous laughter filled the room, and this time nobody began to write right away.

"And I want more volunteers to share this time, too," she said with a twinkle in her eye.

Slowly, tentatively, people began to write. Olivia took a deep breath and then wrote furiously in her notebook the one thing that was bursting to come out.

Bruce was the first to raise his hand to share.

"Mr. Ackerman," Maxine said. "I'm beginning to think you're enjoying this."

Olivia laughed along with everybody else, and Bruce smiled good-naturedly before beginning to read. "Sometimes I have dreams about having sex with Hillary Clinton."

The class erupted in laughter.

"And that's disturbing to you?" Maxine asked when the noise had subsided.

"I'm a Republican."

"Interesting," Maxine said, losing herself in thought for a moment before snapping back and asking for another volunteer.

Olivia raised her hand, introduced herself, then looked down at her notebook and read, "I once walked in on my dad having oral sex with one of his students."

People muttered under their breaths and shook their heads. Even Maxine seemed momentarily taken aback. She looked at Olivia sympathetically. "That's disturbing."

"He teaches seventh grade," Olivia said.

Cries of disgust rang out in the room, and Maxine seemed completely at a loss for words. Trish turned to Olivia with a disbelieving stare.

"I'm kidding," Olivia said.

Maxine shook her head. "That's quite a thing to kid about. You might be even more twisted than I am." She chuckled and gave Olivia an approving glance. "Anyone want to follow that?"

After a moment, a boy across from Olivia raised his hand. He introduced himself as Chuck Garrett, which prompted Maxine to say, "You're up, Chuck," and then apologize immediately. "Totally uncalled for," she said. "Please, go ahead."

Chuck was a rather innocuous-looking boy, the kind you might pass a hundred times and never really notice. Looking down at his notebook, he read, "I sometimes wonder what it would be like to have sex with a sheep."

Bruce laughed out loud, but mostly there was just uncomfortable silence. Was he kidding? Olivia wondered. She exchanged looks with Trish, who seemed to be wondering exactly the same thing.

"Well," Maxine said, with a little smile, "I'm glad you weren't feeling too sheepish to share."

Chuck gave a little smile, and Olivia decided that he was either very disturbed or else a complete genius.

"Now, why did we do that?" Maxine asked. "Why spend the beginning of our first day together reveling in the muck of our deepest, darkest, most depraved thoughts?"

"Because you're a sadist," Bruce said with a smile.

"I've been called worse. Why else?"

"It's a more interesting icebreaker than the human knot," Olivia offered.

"I love the human knot," Trish said.

"And well you should," Maxine said. "Other ideas?"

More answers followed.

"To build community."

"To push us to take risks."

"To generate writing topics."

"To take up time because you forgot to plan for this class."

"Because genius and suffering are inextricably linked," Olivia said.

Maxine's eyes twinkled. "Indeed. Which is why you will all now line up and prepare to be flogged."

The irony of the situation was that nobody seemed to be suffering. Certainly Olivia was feeling better than she could remember having felt in a long time. Publicizing her misfortune had been cathartic; she couldn't wait to begin writing her play in earnest.

"I knew you were a sadist," Bruce said.

"You enjoy saying that, don't you, Mr. Ackerman?" She smiled at him. "Well, maybe you have something worth exploring—a psychological drama that examines the relationship between a sadistic teacher and her masochistic student. It has potential, you know, even if it *has* been done before." She turned to the class. "Finding a subject that's worth writing about is the key to producing anything worthwhile. I can't tell you what that thing is, but I can tell you this. If it's not something that occupies your thoughts for a good portion of each day, then you should probably look somewhere else."

"So basically you're saying we should write about sex," Bruce said.

Most of the students laughed.

"If you feel like you have something deep and penetrating to offer," Maxine returned with a smile.

"I love this lady," Olivia whispered to Trish.

"A lot of writing teachers will tell you to write what you know," Maxine said. "Who can tell me what that means?"

Most of the hands in the class went up, and Maxine called on a girl who had not yet spoken.

"It means that you should write about things you know a lot about because you'll probably have a lot to say and it will be believable."

Maxine nodded. "Anything else?"

"Your writing should be rooted in your own experiences," Chuck said.

"Baa, baa, black sheep," Trish began to sing under her breath, until a laughing Olivia shushed her.

"How many of you already have some idea what you'll be writing your plays about this summer?"

Most of the hands in the room went up.

"And how many of you are planning to write plays that in some way are drawn from your own life experiences?"

Now about half the students, Olivia included, raised their hands. She had not fleshed out all the details, but the premise of her story had been taking shape ever since she had walked in on her father, and she had a title she loved, *Castration Celebration*.

"Here's the thing about writing what you know," Maxine said. "Sometimes you can get so caught up in trying to stay true to your experiences that you start to feel trapped when your story wants to go in another direction." She paused a moment to let this point sink in. "Remember. We're writing fiction in this class, not memoir."

"But isn't art supposed to imitate life?" Bruce challenged.

Oh, shut up, Olivia thought.

"In its broad strokes, perhaps," Maxine agreed. "But art is also a form of creative manipulation."

"I'm confused," the mousy-looking girl said.

"Let's all try something," Maxine said. "Instead of focusing on what we already know, let's take a few minutes to think about what we want to find out. In your notebooks, go ahead and jot down one or two big questions that you don't have the answers to, but that you wish you did."

The first thing Olivia wrote was *Why is my family so dysfunctional?* She stared at her page, trying to think of something else. Everything that came to mind was essentially an offshoot of what she had just written. Come on, she thought, what was something else she might want to figure out? The answer popped into her head, and it took her a little bit by surprise. True, she had brooded about the situation with Max since she had left him the night before, but she had convinced herself that her mind was made up on the subject. Was it possible, after all, that she wasn't so sure? She hesitated, because putting the words on the page would be an admission of something she didn't want to admit. Her pen hovered over her paper, and at last she wrote a single word. *Max?*

"Okay," Maxine said after everyone had finished. "We've done a few things this morning that I hope have gotten you thinking. Now it's time to write. You can use what we just did as a springboard, or you can go off in your own direction." She looked at her watch. "It's ten o'clock. We'll write for an hour and come back together at eleven. If you want to stay here, that's fine. If you want to wander off and find a place outside to work, that's okay, too. Wherever you'll be most productive." She looked around the room. "Questions? Comments? Snide remarks?"

People jumped up and shuffled out of the room. Olivia and Trish walked out into the courtyard. Fifty yards away a group of students was moving around in crazy formations, changing speeds, using their bodies in overly expressive ways. One of the acting classes, no doubt.

"You want to go sit on the stairs?" Trish asked.

"I'm going to go take a quick look at what's going on over there. See if Mimi and Callie are in that class." And Max, she thought, though she kept this to herself.

"I'm going to start writing," Trish said.

"I'll meet you on the stairs." She walked across the courtyard and leaned against a tree with a view of the proceedings. Mimi was there, and Callie, and Max. They were doing an acting exercise where as they moved, the teacher, balding and with a British accent, would call out new directions and they would have to adjust on the spot.

"Suspicious," the teacher said, and immediately the students began to move more cautiously, to glance over their shoulders and cast each other furtive looks.

"Tired," the teacher called. "Nervous." "Dejected." "Amused."

They were good, these student actors, though they tended to exaggerate the traits in similar ways. Max was the best, she noted. His movements and expressions were subtler, but they conveyed so much. And his natural charisma made it hard to look away.

"In love," the teacher called out.

The students began to swoon and cast dreamy, faraway looks. Max looked up and locked eyes with Olivia. He held his hands to his heart and stared at her, love struck.

She shook her head and rolled her eyes, but she felt herself smiling as she walked back to the stairs and sat down next to Trish.

"Do you know how you're going to start your play?" Trish asked, looking up.

Olivia opened her notebook. "I had some ideas, but now I'm not sure." She looked down at the blank page and began to chew on her pen cap.

"Do you think that sheep thing was true?" Trish asked.

Olivia laughed. "I wouldn't be surprised."

"Do all boys think about stuff like that?"

Olivia shrugged. "Who knows?" She looked back across the courtyard, trying to spot Max. "I hope not."

They sat hunched over their notebooks, and Olivia wrote *Castration Celebration* across the top of her page. What could she do to grab readers right away? It had to be something funny and shocking. A song about castration? Maybe, but that would probably work better later in the play. Maybe she could do something with the whole screwing sheep idea. It would be a great way to introduce her male characters and the conversation could be hilarious. She began to feel creative energy pulse through her, and with rising excitement she brought pen to paper and started to write.

CASTRATION CELEBRATION
Act 1, scene 1

(*Curtains open on a small town. A backdrop reveals houses, a school, and a green. A big sign reads* Welcome to New Melon. *The spotlight shines on Biff, Sluggo, and Dick, three teenage boys sitting on one of the stoops.*)

BIFF: All I'm saying is that a sheep wouldn't be so bad. I mean, if you close your eyes, it would probably just feel soft and woolly.

SLUGGO: Do we have to have this conversation again?

BIFF: I'm serious. If I had to choose one animal—

SLUGGO: Dude, I'll give you a hundred bucks if you screw a sheep.

BIFF: A hundred bucks? No way.

SLUGGO: How much then?

BIFF: At least a thousand.

SLUGGO: Where am I gonna get a thousand dollars?

BIFF: Fine, forget the money then. I'll do it·if you whip it out in Ms. Morris's class and jack off on your desk.

SLUGGO: Hold on. You're saying I have to take out my penis in the middle of math class and masturbate on my desk? While she's teaching? That's crazy, man.

BIFF: Dude, I'm talking about screwing a sheep here.

SLUGGO: All right, I'll tell you what. I'll jack off in Ms. Morris's class, but then you've got to screw a sheep and a pig.

BIFF: No way. If I have to screw a sheep and a pig, then you've got to whip it out, jack off on your desk, and sing "God Bless America" while you're doing it.

SLUGGO: If I've got to sing "God Bless America" while I'm jacking off in class, then you've got to screw a sheep, a pig, and Delores Huffenpot.

BIFF (*recoiling*): Brutal.

SLUGGO: Deal or no deal?

BIFF (*reluctantly*): I don't know. You think that's fair, Dick?

DICK (*distracted*): Huh?

BIFF: You think it's fair for me to have to screw a sheep, a pig, and Delores Huffenpot if Sluggo jacks off in class while singing "God Bless America"?

DICK (*shaking his head*): What the hell's the matter with you?

BIFF: What? What did I say?

DICK: Forget it.

(*Dick gets up and begins to pace, and Sluggo and Biff look at each other, confused.*)

SLUGGO: What's the matter, Dick? You having your period or something? I could run over to the store and get you a box of tampons.

DICK: I'm just so sick of it.

SLUGGO: What?

DICK: This. Everything. (*looks earnestly at his two companions*) Don't you ever just want to get away from here?

BIFF: What are you talking about?

DICK: Just get in the car and keep driving.

SLUGGO: Where do you want to go?

DICK: I don't know. It doesn't even matter. Just somewhere else.

BIFF: How about Disney World?

SLUGGO: Come on, Dick. We'll go out tonight, you'll get a little action, and you'll feel much better. Trust me.

BIFF: Man, I hope I get me some action, too.

SLUGGO: See there. We'll find you a girl, and then we'll find Biff a nice woolly sheep.

BIFF: Actually, Sluggo, I was thinking about your mom. She still charge the same rates?

SLUGGO: That wasn't my mom. It was my grandma. Couldn't you tell from the wheelchair and hearing aid?

BIFF (*offering a high five*): Nice one. So what do you fellas say? You ready to hit the town?

DICK: Not tonight, guys.

SLUGGO: Are you serious? We can't go cruising without you.

BIFF: Yeah, come on, Dick. If you don't come, there's no way I'm getting laid.

DICK: You guys don't need me to score with chicks.

SLUGGO: It helps.

DICK: Give me a break. You guys have scored on your own before. Biff, remember when you hooked up with Amber Bloom last month? I wasn't with you then.

BIFF: Yeah, that was awesome.

SLUGGO: You only hooked up with her because she was so drunk she had no idea who you were.

BIFF: I know. Drunk girls rule.

DICK: Look. All you guys need to do is drive around tonight, wait for some really drunk girls to stagger out of a bar, and offer them a ride.

SLUGGO: What about finding Biff a sheep?

BIFF: I told you already. Your mom is woolly enough.

SLUGGO: You really think we'll score tonight without you?

DICK: Just don't talk about sheep. Now get out of here and go bag some chicks.

SLUGGO (*reluctantly*): All right, man. Catch you later, then.

DICK: Later.

(*Sluggo and Biff exit, leaving Dick alone on the front stoop.*)

(*On another stoop we see Jane and Amber. Jane is wearing sweatpants and a sweatshirt and is holding*

a copy of Shakespeare's play Much Ado About Nothing.
Amber is wearing a short skirt, a tight shirt, and
heavy makeup.)

AMBER: Come on, Jane. It will be fun.

JANE (*sarcastically*): It sounds great. I mean, what
could be more exciting than flirting with some
skeevy guy at a liquor store so he'll sell us cheap
beer, then getting puking drunk and making out with
Biff Berchum?

AMBER: That was one time, okay? And I've already
admitted it was a severe lapse in judgment. But
come on, Jane. There are lots of guys out there.
If you'd just dress up a little and put on
some makeup, you could have anyone you
wanted.

JANE (*with fake enthusiasm*): And there's such a
great selection to choose from.

AMBER: Listen to you, Miss Picky. You planning to
hold out for Brad Pitt?

JANE: I don't know. Does he like to read?

AMBER: You can't just stay in every Saturday night.
Everyone goes out.

JANE: Exactly. It's enough that I have to deal with these people during the week.

AMBER: So what are you going to do? Close yourself off in your room and read your Shakespeare for English class? We're going to be doing the play out loud in class, anyway, so you're just going to be reading it twice. I mean, look at the title. *Much Ado About Nothing*. Who wants to waste time reading a book about nothing?

JANE: Remind me again how we're friends.

AMBER: Seriously, we hardly ever hang out, except in school.

JANE: If I go out with you, you're just going to end up hooking up with some guy, anyway.

AMBER: That's not true.

(*Jane gives her a look, and Amber smiles sheepishly.*)

AMBER: So we can do something else, then, just the two of us. See a movie or something.

JANE: No, you go out. Really. I like staying home. (*She holds up her Shakespeare play.*) Besides, I've got old Willy to keep me company.

AMBER: What you need is a young Willy to keep you company.

JANE: Oh my God, do you ever think about anything other than sex?

AMBER: Not really.

JANE: You know, if you didn't look so good in a skirt, I might mistake you for a guy.

AMBER: Why? You think only guys are obsessed with sex? That's like so sexist.

JANE: No it's not. Do you even know what sexist means?

AMBER: What do you mean? Of course I do.

JANE: So explain to me how I'm being sexist.

AMBER: You're saying that only guys can be obsessed with sex. That's like saying that only guys can play football or drive trucks or be president.

JANE: It's true, isn't it?

AMBER (*laughing*): Shut up.

JANE: Well, if we're going by your definition, then aren't you being sexist by only dating guys? I mean, what are you saying—that girls aren't good enough for you?

AMBER: Oh my God, that's totally different.

JANE: How?

AMBER: It just is. And you're not gonna suck me into one of your ridiculous debates.

JANE: You started it.

AMBER: Whatever. So, come on. Are you coming out with me tonight?

JANE (*holding up her play*): I told you. I've already got plans.

AMBER: Loser.

JANE: Sexist.

(*They both start to laugh.*)

AMBER: You sure I can't convince you?

JANE (*standing and bending down to give Amber a hug*): Positive. Just try not to do anything that you'll be too embarrassed to tell me about tomorrow.

(*Amber exits, and music begins.*)

"There's Nothing to Do in New Melon"
(*Jane*)
My name is Jane, and on Saturday night
I usually stay home and read
I tell my friend it's how I want to spend
My time, and it's all I need

In my room, every Saturday night
I play a game of make-believe
Yeah, I'm lonely, but I hope it's only
Till I graduate and get to leave

I dream about the day I get to college
Surrounded by ideas, people seeking knowledge
That's where I'll dare to say goodbye to solitaire
Who wants to play with me?

There's nothing to do in New Melon
It's always the same old thing
Oh, I wish I could find a beautiful mind
And get out of this old routine
I wish I could find a way to beat the grind
Looking for a brand-new scene . . .

(Dick)

My name is Dick, and on Saturday night

I usually hang out with my boys

Get in our cars, drive past the bars

Get drunk and make lots of noise

On the town, every Saturday night

I play a game of make-believe

I try to score, and each time I'm more

Convinced it's not what I need

I don't like it, but I've got my reputation

A whole bunch of groupies who give me validation

My luck, I'm stuck, acting like a dumb fuck

I wish I could just break free

There's nothing to do in New Melon

It's always the same old thing

Oh, I wish I could find a beautiful mind

And get out of this old routine

I wish I could find a way to beat the grind

Looking for a brand-new scene . . .

(Dick and Jane)

There's nothing to do in New Melon

It's always the same old thing

Hey out there, I need someone to share

All my hopes and my dreams

53

(Jane)

I feel as if there's someone out there waiting

(Dick)

All of a sudden my heart is palpitating

(Dick and Jane)

Somewhere, out there, breathing in the same air
When will you come to me?
Somewhere, out there, breathing in the same air
When will you come to me?

(They both turn and walk slowly inside their
respective houses.)

(Curtain)

CHAPTER FIVE

According to Max's therapist, Max's relationship history was not surprising given the fact that his mother had abandoned him as a child. He latched on to girls compulsively, accelerated the process toward intimacy, and walked away from each girlfriend before she had the chance to walk away from him. His therapist was working on this with him, and he had left for the summer determined to break his pattern. What he was not prepared for—because it was a brand-new experience for him—was being flat-out rejected before a relationship had even started. And what made this particular rejection such a hard pill to swallow was his conviction that he and Olivia were perfect for each other.

"Come on," he urged her, walking back from lunch on the third day. "I know we have afternoons free to work, but it's too nice out to stay cooped up in your room writing."

"I just want to get a few more pages knocked out before class tomorrow."

"So write outside, at least," he said as they turned off Elm

Street and into the Old Campus courtyard. "I'll sit with you and give you ideas if you get stuck."

She smiled and shook her head. "No, thanks. You'll just be a distraction."

"I won't, I promise."

She gave him a skeptical look, and he pretended to tape his mouth shut.

"Yeah, right," she said, laughing.

They walked across the courtyard toward their dorm without speaking. It was exciting to Olivia how her play was taking shape. Her characters were charting their own paths, and Dick was emerging as a much more sympathetic character than she ever would have imagined. Maybe being around Max really was affecting her. She looked at him, and he pointed toward the stairs and cocked his eyebrows.

"You can talk," she said.

He exhaled dramatically, like someone coming up for air after being underwater for too long. "Thank you," he gasped.

"Okay," Olivia said with a chuckle. "We can try."

"On the stairs?"

She nodded. "I just have to get my notebook."

They neared the dorm, and Olivia suddenly turned to Max. "Can I ask you something a little bit weird and twisted?"

"I can hardly wait," he said.

She looked away from him and stared down at her feet. "Do you ever fantasize about having sex with a sheep?"

"What?" Max said, laughing.

"I told you it was twisted," she said with a smile.

"Wow," Max said. He gave a little wave to someone in his

acting class, who was passing in the other direction. "I guess I'm more of a goat boy," he said at last.

Olivia nodded and tried to keep a straight face. "Interesting. Any other unusual sexual proclivities?"

"Let me see," Max said, racking his brain for something clever to say. "There's midgets, I guess."

"Midgets?"

"Well, their mouths are a perfect height."

"Oh, of course," she said, smiling slightly and feeling slightly repulsed at the same time. "How silly of me."

"And children's books," Max added as they reached the dorm. "I find books for little children to be highly erotic."

"Stop right there," Olivia said, pausing outside the door. "Farm animals and midgets are one thing, but pedophilia . . ."

"Not *kids,* just kids' books. You remember *Pat the Bunny?*"

"Of course. It's a classic."

He took on a lecherous voice. "Pat the furry bunny. Feel Daddy's scratchy face. Slide your finger through Mommy's ring."

She cracked up. "You didn't just come up with that, did you?"

"No," he admitted. "But it was pretty good the way I slipped it in, right?"

"Interesting choice of words," she said, opening the door and stepping inside.

It took him a moment, and then he smiled. "That was actually unintentional."

"Sure it was," she teased, starting up the stairs. "I'll meet you outside."

Max headed toward his room, thinking he would grab his copy of *On the Road.* He wasn't really reading it, but it was the kind of book that looked cool to be carrying around. Much cooler, at least, than *My Ántonia,* which he had to read over the summer for school. When he opened the door, he found Zeke on his cell phone with a disturbed expression on his face.

"Well— I mean, that's what it is," Zeke said, turning away from Max. "Yeah, I know . . . Six weeks. Listen, I've got to go." He closed his phone and turned back around.

"Everything okay?" Max asked, picking up his book from the desk and flipping it over to read the blurb.

Zeke shrugged. "Just some shit back home."

"What happened?" Max asked, looking up.

Zeke sat on his bed and ran his hands through his hair. "Fucking idiot," he mumbled.

"You sure you're okay?" Max asked.

Zeke looked at him. "My friend Devin stopped going to rehab."

"Is that who you were talking about the other night, who smokes so much pot?"

Zeke nodded. "That's not the issue, though. For him being stoned is normal."

"What's he doing? Coke?"

"Among other things." Zeke looked at a spot on the floor. "He was always on something. Ritalin when he was young and then pills to help him sleep. I never thought it was that big a deal. But then he started with the ecstasy and the painkillers and anything else he could get his hands on."

Max looked at Zeke's pack of rolling papers next to his bed. "So that's why the band broke up?"

"He started coming to rehearsals too fucked up to play, or not coming at all." Zeke shook his head slowly and then looked up at Max. "You know, I thought he was maybe going to pull it together when he went into rehab last month."

"Do his parents know?" Max asked.

Zeke picked up his iPod and began to scroll through. "I don't want to talk about it anymore."

Max watched him for a moment. "I've got to go meet Olivia. You want to come? It's beautiful outside."

"No, thanks," Zeke said, putting his iPod in the dock. Pounding rock guitar blared out.

"Is this the Clash?" Max asked.

Zeke nodded and sat back down on his bed.

Max listened for a few seconds. "I forgot to tell you, Trish was looking for you at lunch. She seemed kind of bummed that you weren't there."

"Whatever," Zeke mumbled, picking up his guitar.

"I think she likes you, dude," Max said.

Zeke ignored the comment and started to play along with the music.

Max opened the door and stood in the doorway, watching Zeke. "You sure you don't want to come?"

Zeke shook his head and continued to play.

Outside the dorm, Olivia was waiting, and when she smiled at him he momentarily forgot about Zeke.

"What are you reading?" she asked.

"*On the Road*," he said, showing her the book and feeling more than a little bit pleased with himself.

She looked at the cover and grimaced. "Oh, I can't stand that book."

"Really?" he said as they headed toward the stairs. "What about *My Ántonia*?"

Two hours later, when Max returned to the room, he found Zeke asleep on his back, fully dressed, with the Grateful Dead playing on the dock. The mingled smell of marijuana and air freshener wafted through the room.

Max closed the door quickly and stood looking at his roommate. "Jesus," he said, laughing. "You need to get out and get yourself some fresh air." He leaned over Zeke. "Wake up," he whispered.

Zeke grunted and turned over on his stomach.

"I'm going to have to jump on you," Max said.

Zeke did not respond.

"Okay," Max said, walking to the foot of the bed. "One, two, three," and with that he launched himself on top of his sleeping roommate.

The effect was cataclysmic.

"What the fuck?" Zeke screamed, upending Max and jumping out of bed.

Max shook himself off and smiled. "You were so cute I couldn't resist."

"That's so not cool," Zeke said, glaring at him.

"I'm sorry," Max said, laughing. He held open his arms and took a step forward. "How about a hug?"

"Stay away from me," Zeke said, retreating.

They stood facing each other, Max smiling, Zeke looking thoroughly pissed off.

"So I guess a blow job is out of the question," Max said.

"You're sick."

"How about some cuddling?"

Zeke shook his head. "What the hell's wrong with you?"

"I've just got a lot of pent-up sexual energy."

"So go whack off or something. Jesus." He sat back down on his bed, then reached over and took his water bottle off the dresser.

"I might," Max said, reaching into his closet and grabbing his Frisbee. "You want to go outside and toss this around a bit?"

"No."

"Come on," Max said. "Don't you like playing Frisbee when you're high?"

Zeke sat back on his bed and rubbed his eyes. "Why the fuck did you wake me up?"

Max shrugged. "I don't know. Did you really want to sleep all afternoon?"

"Yeah, I did." He lay back down and stared up at the ceiling.

Max sat on his bed and tossed the Frisbee a few times to himself before putting it back in the closet. "So what's going to happen with Devin?" he asked.

"I still don't want to talk about it," Zeke said irritably.

Max nodded and sat back on his bed. He knew he should spend some time memorizing lines for class, but the heat in the room was sapping his desire to do anything. Unbuckling his sandals, he lay back on his pillow.

"We should buy a fucking fan," he said.

As he felt himself starting to drift off, Olivia sat at her computer upstairs, typing away furiously.

CASTRATION CELEBRATION
Act 1, scene 2

(*A classroom. The teacher is a young man, recently graduated from college, and he stands in front of the room addressing a group of largely uninterested students.*)

TEACHER: Okay, class, open up your plays. *Much Ado About Nothing,* act 1, scene 1. I need eight actors for this scene, but two of the parts are tiny. I'll probably need some girls to take guy parts, because all the parts are men except Beatrice. Any volunteers? (*Nobody raises a hand.*) Oh, come on, guys, this is Shakespeare. (*Still no one volunteers.*) Well, then, I guess I'll just have to assign parts.

JANE (*raising her hand*): I'll play Beatrice.

TEACHER: Excellent. Can I get someone to play Benedick? It's a classic battle-of-the-sexes scene between these two characters.

BIFF: Did you say sex? (*Much of the class starts to laugh.*) I'll volunteer for sex. (*more laughter*)

DICK: Shut up, Biff. (*raising his hand*) I'll do it.

TEACHER (*smiling*): Great. Now who else will take a part?

(*Students volunteer for the remaining parts.*)

TEACHER: All right, then. Actors, front and center.

(*The play begins, and the actors stumble through their lines, with the exceptions of Dick and Jane, who play their parts brilliantly.*)

JANE (*as Beatrice*): I wonder that you will still be talking, Signor Benedick: nobody marks you.

DICK (*as Benedick*): What! my dear Lady Disdain, are you yet living?

JANE (*as Beatrice*): Is it possible Disdain should die while she hath such meet food to feed it as Signor Benedick? Courtesy itself must convert to disdain, if you come in her presence.

DICK (*as Benedick*): Then is courtesy a turncoat. But it is certain I am loved of all ladies, only you excepted; and I would I could find in my heart that I had not a hard heart, for, truly, I love none.

JANE (*as Beatrice*): A dear happiness to women: they would else have been troubled with a pernicious suitor. I thank God and my cold blood, I am of your humor for that: I had rather hear my dog bark at a crow than hear a man swear he loves me.

BIFF (*interrupting the play*): What's going on? I don't get it.

TEACHER: They're insulting each other. Quiet now. Listen.

DICK (*as Benedick*): God keep your ladyship still in that mind; So some gentleman or other shall 'scape a predestinate scratched face.

JANE (*as Beatrice*): Scratching could not make it worse, an 'twere such a face as yours were.

DICK (*as Benedick*): Well, you are a rare parrot-teacher.

JANE (*as Beatrice*): A bird of my tongue is better than a beast of yours.

DICK (*as Benedick*): I would my horse had the speed of your tongue, and so good a continuer. But keep your way, i' God's name; I have done.

JANE (*as Beatrice*): You always end with a jade's trick: I know you of old.

(*The teacher begins to clap, and the whole class follows suit. Jane and Dick make eye contact, smile, and turn away from each other to face the class. The bell rings and students rush off. Dick comes up beside Jane as they exit the classroom.*)

DICK: Hey.

JANE: Oh, hi.

DICK: You were really good up there.

JANE: Thanks. So were you.

DICK: I guess it's not such a stretch for me to play a totally obnoxious guy.

JANE: I guess not.

DICK (*smiling*): Ouch.

JANE (*also smiling*): Sorry.

DICK: It's okay. I deserve it.

(*Jane shuffles things around in her book bag.*)

JANE: Where did you learn to act like that?

DICK (*shrugs*): I don't know. When I was little I used to put on shows all the time, and I would play every part. *Three Little Pigs, Little Red Riding Hood, The Wizard of Oz.* My mom always said I was a born actor.

JANE: You did *The Wizard of Oz* by yourself? That's impressive.

DICK: You should have seen me as the Wicked Witch. (*in the witch's voice*) I'll get you my pretty . . . and your little dog, too!

JANE (*laughs*): Not bad. I used to have nightmares about the Wicked Witch when I was little. And those flying monkeys terrified me.

DICK: You want to hear something weird? I wasn't scared of the witch or the monkeys, but Clifford totally freaked me out.

JANE: Clifford? The big red dog?

DICK: He wasn't big. He was enormous. I used to have nightmares where he would come through the window of my room while I was sleeping and carry me off to the moon.

JANE: That is weird.

DICK: You know, children's books aren't nearly as innocent as they seem. Take any book from when you were little and look at it again and you'll see.

JANE: Oh, come on.

DICK: It's true. Do you remember the book *Pat the Bunny*?

JANE: Of course. It's a classic.

DICK: Have you ever thought about what that book is really about?

JANE: It's not about anything. It's a book for babies.

DICK (*miming the actions he recites in a lewd, suggestive manner*): Pat the furry bunny. Feel Daddy's scratchy face. Slide your finger through Mommy's ring.

JANE: Oh, that's horrible.

DICK: How big is bunny? Sooo big.

JANE (*laughing*): Okay, that is really disturbing.

DICK: And what about Winnie-the-Pooh?

JANE: What about him?

DICK: There's a whole chapter about him getting stuck in Rabbit's hole.

JANE: Okay, that's just ridiculous.

DICK (*smiling*): You know, it's strange that we've been in the same class all these years, and this is the first time we've ever really talked to each other.

JANE: You and your friends aren't exactly the most inviting group of people.

DICK: I know, right? But I'm surprised I haven't noticed you before. (*He stares at her, realizing for the first time how attractive she is.*)

JANE (*made uncomfortable by his stare*): Yeah, well, I keep a kind of low profile.

DICK: But you were the first person to volunteer for a part today.

JANE: I couldn't just sit back and watch Shakespeare get mangled. I mean, come on. Did you hear Jerry

keep pronouncing the "g" in *signor*? (*imitating him*)
Sig-noor Benedick, Sig-noor Benedick.

DICK (*laughing*): And can you imagine if Biff had
played Benedick?

JANE: Can he even read?

DICK (*laughs*): Come on—

JANE: Sorry.

DICK: It's okay. I like a girl with an edge to her.
(*stops and looks at her*) Hey, what are you doing
Saturday night?

JANE (*flustered*): Saturday night? This Saturday
night? Nothing. I mean, I don't know. Usually I stay
home and read.

DICK: You want to do something?

JANE (*regaining her composure*): What, drive around
with you and your friends? No, thanks.

DICK: No. Not that. Just you and me.

JANE: And do what?

DICK: I don't know. (*thinking*) We could go bowling.

JANE (*laughing*): Bowling?

DICK: Why not? Shakespeare used to bowl all the time.

JANE: Was he any good?

DICK: Terrible. That's why he decided to be a writer instead.

JANE (*shaking her head*): The things the history books leave out.

DICK: Tell me about it. Like I bet you didn't know that Abraham Lincoln's real name was Abraham Goldstein, but he didn't think he could win as a Jew, so he changed his name.

JANE: How was his bowling game?

DICK: Not very good. Andrew Johnson, on the other hand . . . that guy could roll. Second-best celebrity bowler in history after Benito Mussolini.

JANE: You're really a storehouse of useless information, aren't you?

DICK: I do my best. I actually know how to say "scrotum" in five languages. You want to hear?

JANE: Not really.

DICK: No, listen. Scroto, escroto, skrotum, le scrotum, and balzac.

JANE: Balzac? You're making that up.

DICK: No, it's Dutch. Really.

JANE: I don't know whether to be impressed or seriously concerned.

DICK: You know, it's not easy growing up named Dick. You end up with an unhealthy preoccupation with your genitals.

JANE: Thus your desire to roll big heavy balls at penis-shaped pins.

DICK (*laughing*): Exactly. So what do you say? You want to come bowling Saturday night?

JANE: I'll think about it. (*She smiles and walks to another part of the stage.*)

(*same music from earlier*)

(*Dick*)
Her name is Jane, and on Saturday night

I'm gonna take her out to bowl
She's really witty and I think she's really pretty
I was broken, but with her I feel whole

Suddenly there's something new in New Melon
I don't have to drive around acting like a felon
Sick heal, fake real, Depression now a New Deal
I think that I might be in love

(Jane)
His name is Dick, and on Saturday night
He's gonna take me out to bowl
He acts all tough, but I see that it's a bluff
I was broken, but with him I feel whole

Suddenly there's something new in New Melon
I'm charting a new course, a modern-day Magellan
Trapped free, I we, no more being lonely
I think that I might be in love

(Dick and Jane)
Trapped free, I we, no more being lonely
I think that I might be in love

(Curtain)

CHAPTER SIX

The next Sunday at two-thirty in the afternoon, Olivia walked downstairs with a completed first act in hand and knocked on Max and Zeke's door. She had been hiding out a lot in her suite the past few days, mostly to write without interruption, but also because she was afraid that if she kept flirting with Max she might lose her resolve to stay single. Indeed, the only reason she was here now was that she needed to talk to Zeke.

Still, if she was being completely honest with herself, she was a little disappointed not to see Max when Zeke opened the door. As much as she hated to admit it, flirting with Max was fun, and their banter always left her charged to write. She stepped inside and looked around the room.

"Max isn't here," Zeke said, "but he should be back soon."

"I actually came to see you." She noticed his guitar on the bed. "Were you practicing?"

He shook his head. "Just messing around."

She sniffed the air and gave Zeke a disbelieving stare.

"What?" he said.

She grinned. "The air freshener doesn't really work."

Zeke shrugged. "Whatever." He sat on his bed and began to tune his guitar.

Olivia noted the pair of boxer shorts with penguins printed on them left lying out on Max's bed and smiled before turning her attention back to Zeke.

"So I was talking to Trish," she said, "and she was telling me that you write a lot of the music you play yourself."

"Some of it," Zeke said.

She watched him tune his final string. "Do you have any interest in working with me on my musical? I'm writing the play and the lyrics for class. I really want someone to write the music for me."

"What's it about?" he asked, strumming a chord and then tightening his D string.

"I've only written the first act. You can look at the opening song if you want."

"I don't know," he said. "I don't really like musicals, to be honest."

"I thought you wrote one with Trish."

He shrugged. "That was for a school assignment."

"I'm sure this is totally different from what you wrote for school. Just read the beginning." She held out the papers in her hand and sat down next to him as he started to read.

He came to the bottom of the first page and looked at her with a smile. "You're writing this for class?"

Olivia nodded, feeling a surge of hope. "So what do you say?"

He continued reading. "What kind of music would you want?"

"Mostly rock, I think, but it doesn't all have to be one style. You could look at the lyrics and tell me what you think."

He leafed through the pages until he got to the first song and started to read more carefully.

"Plus," she said, "for some of the songs I might use music that already exists, so it shouldn't be too much work."

"I don't know," he said, eyes still on the page. "I guess I could try."

"You will?" she said excitedly. "You can keep that copy. It's the whole first act."

The door opened, and Max entered. "Now *that* was a fantastic dump I just—" He noticed Olivia and pulled up short, a look of horror washing over his face.

"Charming," she said.

"You have to warn me when we have company," he said to Zeke.

"She just showed up."

"So," Olivia said, standing and grinning hugely, "do guys always talk about their bowel movements like that, or is it just one of your own little idiosyncrasies?"

"No, it's pretty standard fare," he said, recovering. "Like the way girls always talk about their periods."

She laughed.

"Then again, boys sometimes talk about girls' periods, too," he added.

"Jesus," Zeke mumbled, turning away.

"Let me ask you something." Max's voice took on a playful quality. "Is it true that if a group of girls lives together for long enough, they all start having their periods at the same time?"

"No," Olivia said. "I'm pretty sure that's just a myth."

"Really? I thought it was like some hormonal thing."

Olivia opened the door. "Well, if we all start to menstruate together, I'll be sure to let you know so you can stay far away."

She walked out, and once she did, Zeke looked at Max and shook his head. "Do I really need to see that?"

Max shrugged. "She started it."

Zeke put the script Olivia had given him on his desk facedown.

"Have you seen *The Shining*?" Max asked.

"Yeah, why?"

Max took on the voice of Danny Torrance. "Redrum. Redrum. Redrum."

"Oh, Jesus," Zeke said with a laugh.

"All right, which would you choose?" Max asked. "Being stuck with Jack Nicholson in *The Shining,* or being stuck with a group of girls all having their periods?"

"Jack Nicholson. Definitely."

"I'd take the girls," Max said. "I've heard they're hornier when they're having their periods."

"You'd have sex with a girl when she's all bloody?"

"Definitely. It would be nice and lubricated."

"You're out of control," Zeke said, sitting on his bed and beginning to finger the strings on his guitar.

Max watched him for a moment. "I heard a story about a guy who went down on his girlfriend while she was having her period."

Zeke stopped playing. "That's just nasty."

"You know that book *Twilight*?" Max asked.

"I've heard of it."

"It's about this vampire who hooks up with a teenage chick. They never do more than kiss, but I was thinking if he ever went down on her while she was having her period it would be like winning the fucking lottery."

"This is what you spend your time thinking about?"

"It's like that old commercial," Max said. He began to sing the jingle: "Two great tastes that taste great together—Reese's Peanut Butter Cups."

Zeke shook his head and began to play a blues riff.

"Hey, you know what would be hilarious?" Max said, his eyes lighting up. "If we wrote a song and sent it to the author."

Zeke smiled and continued to play.

"I'm serious. Do you know 'Sunday Bloody Sunday'?"

"The U2 song? I'm sure I can figure it out."

"Do it. I'll add lyrics."

Zeke nailed the chords immediately, and after listening for a few seconds, Max jumped in and began to improvise. They went through a few rounds, and then Max pulled out his notebook and wrote what he had come up with.

"Okay," he said to Zeke. "Let's try from the beginning."

I met a girl named Bella Swan

She had her period

She had a tampon on

Told her

Told her she could take it out

Told her to take it out

'Cause tonight

I will drink your blood tonight

Other drinks, they never quench my thirst

But bloody Bella makes me want to go headfirst

I go crazy for her smell

It must be heaven

But I'm going straight to hell

Bella, Bloody Bella

Bella, Bloody Bella

Bella, Bloody Bella

Zeke played a little closing riff and gave a final big strum to top it off, snapping his D string in the process.

"Fuck," he said, unwinding the broken string.

"So how come Olivia was here?" Max asked. He hadn't seen her much the past few days and had started wondering whether she was purposely trying to avoid him.

Zeke pulled the string loose. "She's writing a musical and wants me to do the music."

"Are you going to do it?"

"I don't know. I fucking hate musicals."

Max laughed. "So, what's it about?"

Zeke rifled through his guitar case. "I only read the beginning."

"Are these the songs?" Max asked, picking the sheaf of papers off the desk and flipping it over.

Zeke nodded. "She left it for me to read."

Max carried it to his bed and sat down. "You mind if I read it?"

"*I* don't care," Zeke said. "I don't know about Olivia."

Max began to read and his eyes popped wide. "Holy shit," he said, laughing. "She was asking me about this the other day."

"What? About fucking sheep?"

"Uh-huh," Max said without looking up.

Zeke watched for a few moments, and then grabbed his keys and wallet. "I'm going to Cutler's to get another string." He walked to the door. "Just leave that on my desk when you finish."

Max looked up briefly, nodded, and returned to the script. Reading Olivia's work felt intensely intimate, like peeking inside her head without her knowing. Was Jane supposed to be her? It would make sense, and then Amber could be based on Mimi. The boys were more difficult. Who acted like that? Was it possible that he could be Dick? He continued to read, and felt his excitement rising as he moved through the second scene. Dick was using his words, the exact same ones he had used with Olivia a few days earlier. And now, here were Dick and Jane starting to fall for each other. Did it mean that Olivia actually liked him? That all her talk of not wanting to get involved wasn't, in fact, true?

He came to the end and immediately went back and read the whole act through a second time. Maybe he was reading too much into it. It's just a play, he thought, and the whole thing could be entirely made up. Still, it was surprising that Olivia was writing a love story. And wasn't it supposed to be true that art imitated life? It would be interesting to see how the plot developed.

* * *

Upstairs in the girls' suite, Olivia was wondering the same thing. Now that Zeke had agreed to try writing music, she was eager to push on and get a few more songs finished. Opening her notebook, she scrawled *SONG IDEAS* on the top of a clean page and began jotting down some thoughts:

"Amber Is a Boy's Best Friend"
    Humorously chronicle her sordid past—
maybe start innocent and get progressively
more outrageous (threesome, bestiality, Biff)—
never able to satisfy her craving—funny
and sad

"My Son Will Go Out Tomorrow"
    Humorous takeoff on Annie—Dick's father
singing proudly about how his son is going to
score and reminiscing about his own glory days

"A Dick Is a Dick"
    Play with double entendres—cocky, has a
big head, pushy, why does it have to be so hard?

Mimi burst into the room. "Oh my God," she said, "you'll never believe what happened in class today." She slipped out of her flip-flops and came up beside Olivia. "We were doing this activity where we had to become someone else in the room, and Callie chose Max, and it was so funny because she was flirting with all the girls, and then she went up to the girl who was playing me, and they, like, pretended to make out. And Max was playing the teacher and he started pretending that it was getting him really horny and he started to say, 'Oh, yeah, baby,' only he did it in the teacher's accent, and we all started cracking up, and even the teacher thought it was funny." She finished talking and plopped down on her bed.

"Is he really that slimy, your teacher?" Olivia asked.

"Ewww, no. That would be so gross. He's like fifty years old."

The same age as my father, thought Olivia grimly. She had a sudden image of her father flirting with Mimi and felt like she might be sick.

"Have you ever dated someone older?" she asked.

Mimi considered the question. "I went out with a senior my sophomore year, who took me to the prom. And I've hooked up with some older boys, but I didn't really date them."

"How old was the oldest guy you ever hooked up with?"

She thought for a moment. "I don't really know. I kissed this guy at a party who said he was in college, but I think he might have been older. He was kind of a jerk, actually."

"What happened?"

She shook her head ruefully. "He got angry because I wouldn't sleep with him. The whole thing was stupid." She got up from her bed and walked into the bathroom, leaving Olivia to imagine the story for herself.

CASTRATION CELEBRATION
Act 2, scene 1

(The same setting as the beginning of the play.
Loud voices and laughter. Amber comes running

onstage, *with Charlie, who looks to be about thirty, chasing after her.*)

CHARLIE: Where are we going?

AMBER: You'll see.

CHARLIE (*stopping and catching his breath*): I'm worn out. You've been running me around all night.

AMBER: Aren't you having fun?

CHARLIE: I need a cigarette. (*takes one out and lights it*)

AMBER (*coming over to him*): You know you shouldn't smoke. It's bad for you. (*takes a cigarette from his pack, then takes his lit cigarette and uses it to light her own*)

CHARLIE: But you smoke anyway.

AMBER (*inhaling, then exhaling smoke*): I do a lot of things that are bad for me.

(*They stand there smoking.*)

CHARLIE: You still haven't told me your name.

AMBER: Does it matter?

CHARLIE: You're something else, you know that? You could make a guy crazy chasing after you.

AMBER (*dropping her cigarette and pressing up against Charlie*): What about you? Am I making you crazy?

CHARLIE (*taking her head in his hands and kissing her hard on the mouth*): You're making me insane.

(*They begin to kiss more passionately. Amber pulls away.*)

CHARLIE (*confused*): What's the matter?

AMBER: I'm going home now. Good night. (*She starts to walk off.*)

CHARLIE: Wait. (*He catches her by the arm.*) What's going on? Did I do something wrong?

AMBER (*shaking her head*): I'm just tired.

CHARLIE: Well, let me walk with you at least. (*He puts his arm around her.*)

AMBER (*shrugging off his arm*): Don't.

CHARLIE (*angrily*): What the hell? You don't throw
yourself all over a guy, and then just walk away.

AMBER: Look, Charlie, you seem like a nice guy. So
don't be an asshole, okay?

CHARLIE: Me? An asshole? You're the asshole. What's
your problem, anyway?

AMBER: I'm an asshole.

CHARLIE (*shaking his head*): You're lucky I'm a nice
guy. One of these days you're gonna get yourself
into some serious trouble acting like that. Goddamn
cock-tease. (*Walks off, nearly bumping into Jane,
who has just walked onstage. Jane sees Amber and
hurries over to her.*)

JANE: Who was that guy?

AMBER (*in no mood to talk*): Nobody. Just someone I
met tonight.

JANE: He looked angry.

AMBER: He'll get over it.

JANE: How old was he? Thirty?

AMBER (*shrugging*): Maybe.

JANE: Jesus, Amber. You better be careful. One of these guys might be a serial rapist or something.

AMBER: He was harmless. He had a Mickey Mouse key chain.

JANE: He's probably a pedophile.

AMBER (*angrily*): Why do you assume that anyone I go out with is some kind of criminal? You think your precious boyfriend is the only nice guy out there?

JANE (*stunned by Amber's outburst*): No, of course not. I'm sorry, Amber, I was just kidding around.

AMBER: Well, it's not funny. (*She starts to cry.*)

(*Jane steps forward and hugs her, and Amber continues to cry into Jane's shoulder.*)

JANE (*gently*): It's okay. Everything's gonna be okay.

AMBER (*gathering herself*): I'm sorry. I don't know what's wrong with me.

JANE: Do you feel like talking about it?

AMBER: I'm fine.

JANE: You sure?

AMBER (*nods and forces a smile*): What about you?
Didn't you go out with Dick?

JANE (*smiling*): We went bowling. I got a strike and
two spares.

AMBER: Hey, you're getting pretty good.

JANE: Well, Dick finally showed me the right way to
hold the ball.

AMBER (*smiling lasciviously*): I'll bet he did.

JANE: Oh my God, you're so perverted. Tell me again
how we're friends.

AMBER: Oh, don't act all pure and innocent. You and
Dick have been all over each other for the past
three weeks.

JANE (*blushing*): We have not.

AMBER: Yeah, right. Holding hands in the hallway and
kissing by the lockers and cuddling on the couches
in the lounge. It's like, get a room already.

JANE: Is it really that bad?

AMBER: It's nauseating.

JANE: Oh God. I'm turning into the kind of person I used to have nightmares about.

AMBER: Relax. It's kind of cute, actually. I mean, two people so in love.

JANE: Shut up.

AMBER: I'm serious. Love is a hard thing to find these days.

JANE: What are you talking about? You fall in love almost every day.

AMBER: That's not love. And every guy I'm into turns out to be a disaster.

JANE: You know what I think? I think you purposely chase after guys you know aren't right for you so if things don't work out you won't get hurt.

AMBER: Is that your professional opinion?

JANE: You don't agree with me?

AMBER: No.

JANE: So what do you think, then?

AMBER: I think when I was born, my father made a deal with the devil. He could screw around all he wanted, but I would be cursed never to find true love.

JANE: I thought you said your father was the devil.

AMBER: Good point. Maybe I'm just unlucky.

JANE: You think?

AMBER (*starts to sing*):

"Unlucky in Love"

They say that love is blind
And it must be true
Because each time I try to love
I end up black and blue

Must love be so painful
So full of push and shove
I guess I'm just unlucky
When it comes to love

I fell for Mel,

His smell cast a spell,

But oh it was hell

Let me tell you

When I found him in bed

With a fellow named Fred,

Said he wanted to try something new

I might have been willing to stay

But he brought home a new guy the very next day

Oh, I'm unlucky in love

Yeah, I'm unlucky in love

You know Tiny Tim,

Well, it sure wasn't him,

Dim, yes, but most well-endowed

Hung like a horse,

Oh the brute force,

When I lay back and had my fields plowed

If only he wasn't so dirty

If only his IQ was more than thirty

Oh, I'm unlucky in love

Yeah, I'm unlucky in love

Why can't I find a guy

Who's worth my full deposit

No skeletons in the closet

Has everything I need

I want a guy to buy

I've had enough bad rentals

I'm starting to go mental

I want to plant some seeds

Stan had a van

And a Florida tan,

What a man, if he only had hair

I had to abort

A courtship with Stuart

When I found a wart you know where

I dated Tom, Rick, and Harry

One loved his mom, one was sick, one married

Oh, I'm unlucky in love

Yeah, I'm unlucky in love

I'm unlucky in love

Yeah, I'm unlucky in love

JANE: What's the big deal if a guy loves his mom? That sounds like a good thing.

AMBER: Not the way he loved her.

JANE: Ewww. Don't tell me.

AMBER: One time he called out her name while we were—

JANE: Stop. I don't want to know.

AMBER: Do you think there's something wrong with me, Jane?

JANE: What do you mean?

AMBER: I'm always throwing myself all over guys I barely know. It's like I need sexual attention to feel like I have any self-worth, but I always end up feeling more depressed and miserable. You saw how I was tonight. (*puts her head in her hands*) It's like I've turned into a female version of my father.

JANE: You're nothing like your father.

AMBER: Oh God, I don't want to see him if he's home tonight. Can I sleep at your house?

JANE: Of course. (*playfully*) Sam will be excited.

AMBER: Shut up.

JANE: You know he's in love with you, right?

AMBER: He's your brother, Jane, and he's like thirteen. I'm not that depraved.

JANE: You could make a young boy very happy.

AMBER: Oh my God, you're worse than I am. Can we just go to your house and like watch a movie or something?

JANE: Sure. Have you seen *Harold and Maude*?

AMBER: I don't think so. What's it about?

JANE: It's kind of an unconventional love story.

AMBER: That sounds good.

JANE: Yeah. It's one of Sam's favorites.

(*Curtain*)

CHAPTER SEVEN

It was almost eleven o'clock, and Max was feeling randy. The curfew did not restrict students from visiting other rooms, so Max headed upstairs and knocked on the girls' door.

They were all there, hanging out in the common room. Max settled himself on a couch next to Mimi, who had patted the seat next to her and told him to come sit. He would have preferred to sit next to Olivia, but he wasn't complaining. Just being here with four girls, the air felt charged with erotic possibility.

"What's Zeke up to?" Trish asked, trying to sound as casual as possible.

"He's actually working on the music for your play," Max said to Olivia. "I tried to get him to come up with his guitar, but he didn't want to."

"The stuff he's writing is amazing," Olivia said to Trish. "He played some for me before."

"I told you," Trish said.

"Hey," Mimi said, looking meaningfully at Trish. "Maybe he wants some company downstairs."

"Shut up, Mimi," she said, blushing. "Olivia, read us the scene you were working on in class today. She has this one song where the guys are singing about how horny they are. I thought I was going to die I was laughing so hard."

"I'd like to hear it," Max said.

Olivia shook her head. "I don't think so." The song—the whole scene actually—was about as obscene and inappropriate as anything she had ever written.

"Come on." Mimi clapped. "Please."

"We don't need a song," Callie said. "Everyone knows boys walk around like dogs in heat."

"Woof, woof," Max barked.

"Hey," Olivia said to Callie, trying to divert attention from her play. "I heard you did a pretty good imitation of Max the other day."

"Oh my God," Mimi said. "Max, do your imitation of Mr. Wells."

Max hesitated, but Mimi grabbed his hand and pulled him up.

"Get up," she said to the other girls. "We'll pretend to be students in the class."

They stood, and Max eyed them lecherously. "All right then, class," he said in a dead-on impression of Mr. Wells. "Stand straight, arms by your sides, breasts thrust out."

The girls cracked up.

"Focus," Max yelled. "The professional actor does not laugh in the middle of a scene, unless that scene calls for laughter." He glared at the girls, who struggled to keep straight faces.

"We will now commence to exercise our tongues," he said.

Trish lost it first, and then, like dominoes, each of the others fell into a fit of hysterics.

When they sat back down, Olivia noticed that Mimi had moved closer to Max and was sitting so their bodies were touching. Max didn't seem to mind, nor did he object to the fact that she kept finding reasons to touch him as they talked.

Hussy, she thought, and then scolded herself for feeling jealous. She could have gone out with him if she had wanted and she had chosen not to. Why should she care if he and Mimi hooked up? But obviously she did care. She thought about what was happening in her play. Maxine had said to write what you want to find out, and all of a sudden her main character was throwing caution to the wind and letting herself fall for a boy, who would probably be nothing but trouble.

She watched Mimi curl her legs under her on the couch and lean into Max.

"I'm going to say good night," Olivia said, getting up and stretching.

Max stared at her and frowned. "Already? It's still early."

"It's almost midnight," she said, looking at her watch.

He stood up. "Well, I guess I should head downstairs."

"No, stay a while," Mimi said, taking his arm and gently pulling him back on the couch.

He met Olivia's eyes, and she flashed him a tight smile. "Good night, everyone," she said. As she disappeared into the bathroom, Mimi melded herself into Max's body.

"I'm going to go get ready for bed, too," Callie said. "You coming, Trish?" She gave her roommate a knowing look.

Trish looked at Mimi curled up next to Max on the couch and stood up. "Good night," she said, walking into her room, staring at herself in the mirror and pinching the fat on her stomach.

Max understood what was happening, and he felt a mixture of nervous excitement and uncertainty. He was not new at this, and every signal Mimi was throwing out was for him to lean over and start kissing her as soon as the coast was clear. A part of him wanted to, but could he do that when Olivia was the one he really liked? Even if this was just a casual hookup, the girls would talk, and then the whole thing would start to get really complicated. Why couldn't it be Olivia who was out here with him now?

It took a few minutes for everybody to finish in the bathroom and close bedroom doors, but as soon as they did, Mimi moved even closer and began to trace her fingers up his arm. "Hi," she said.

Her breasts were pushing into him and he felt himself becoming slightly aroused. Should he kiss her? What if somebody walked in? He pulled back and looked at the closed doors.

"They won't come out," Mimi said.

"Are you sure?"

"Come on." She took him by the hand, led him into the bathroom, and locked the door. "Now," she said, turning and facing him.

His mind felt strangely blank as they kissed, and he was only vaguely aware of her hands pulling him closer into her. After a few seconds, she stopped and took a step back.

"What's the matter?" she asked.

"What do you mean?"

"Were you even kissing me?"

"I thought I was."

She shook her head. "It didn't feel like it."

It was true, he realized, that his head and heart were someplace else. "I'm just tired, I guess," he said.

She smiled sympathetically. "I know what it is. You like Olivia, don't you?"

He looked away, embarrassed.

"It's okay," she said. "I kind of had a feeling from the first night." She took his hand and waited for him to look at her. "Really, don't worry."

"I feel bad."

"It's okay," Mimi said. "You're not a very good kisser, anyway."

Max laughed. "That was pretty bad, wasn't it?"

"It was kind of like kissing a dead fish."

"Ouch. And now you're going to spend the summer thinking I'm the world's worst kisser." He shook his head in mock despair.

"Don't worry. I won't tell Olivia."

"Don't tell her about any of this, okay?" Max said.

"I won't," she said without a trace of hurt or anger.

He opened his arms and hugged her. "You're the best, you know that?"

She pulled away and smiled. "Too bad you'll never find out."

After Max left, Mimi eased open her bedroom door, but found Olivia awake, hunched over in bed writing.

"You're still up," she said.

Olivia closed her notebook. "Did Max leave?"

"Yeah." She grabbed a towel and her toothpaste and tried to avoid eye contact. "I'm going to go wash up for bed," she said.

Olivia watched her hurry out. Had anything happened? A part of her was dying to know, and another part of her was working hard to convince herself that she shouldn't care. How long had it been since she left them? Only about twenty minutes, so not enough time for anything major. Should she ask Mimi when she came back? Or would that make it obvious that she was interested? Maybe she could just joke about how touchy-feely they had been. God, what the hell was the matter with her? She was turning into the kind of girl she would normally mock.

As it turned out, Olivia did not have to say anything. With the lights out and both girls in bed, Mimi opened the conversation.

"Max totally likes you," she said.

Olivia felt a shiver run through her body. "Did he say something to you?"

"It was more the way he acted."

Olivia turned on her side, so she was facing Mimi's bed.

"Do you like him?" Mimi asked after a few seconds had passed.

"I'm off boys this summer, remember?"

"You're sure?"

"Look," Olivia said a bit testily, "if you're asking if it's okay for you to go after him, I already told you it's fine." She caught herself, and her voice took on a more playful quality. "I mean, you guys looked to be getting along pretty well tonight yourselves. I almost thought you might start making out right in front of us."

Mimi giggled. "Shut up, we so were not."

"I half expected to wake up this morning and find the two of you naked on the couch together."

"Ewww!" Mimi screeched.

"I'm just playing with you."

"Play with yourself," Mimi said, and then, as Olivia laughed, added, "that's not what I meant."

"So *nothing* happened between you and Max tonight?" Olivia asked.

Mimi hesitated. "No, not really."

"You can tell me," Olivia said. "I don't care."

"Nothing happened."

"Whatever," Olivia said.

They were both quiet after that, and Olivia turned onto her back and closed her eyes.

"Okay," Mimi said, as the silence stretched out. "Here's what happened. I kissed him, but he didn't kiss me back."

"I don't care," Olivia said. "Really."

Mimi sat up in bed. "Are you angry?"

"Why would I be angry? I was the one who tried to pimp you off on him in the first place."

Mimi laughed. "Don't tell Max I told you. I promised him I wouldn't."

"I thought you said he didn't do anything."

"He didn't."

"So why would he care?"

"I don't know. He just said not to tell you."

Olivia turned over and stared at the wall. She didn't need this kind of distraction. Let Max and Mimi do whatever they wanted. She was here this summer to write, and to hell with everything else.

CASTRATION CELEBRATION
Act 2, scene 2

(*Dick is at his locker. Sluggo and Biff approach and stand menacingly on either side of him. Nobody else is in the hallway.*)

SLUGGO: We need to talk, man. (*Biff nods.*)

DICK (*looking from one to the other and registering the serious looks on their faces*): Okay. What's up?

SLUGGO: Me and Biff, we weren't gonna say anything, but you've been acting a little (*pauses, searching for the right word*) strange lately. (*Biff nods.*)

DICK: What do you mean strange?

BIFF: Like a faggot.

SLUGGO: Easy, Biff. (*addressing Dick*) You know. Acting all goody-goody in class, going bowling on Saturday night, following Jane around like some whipped puppy.

BIFF: Bowling is for faggots.

SLUGGO: Biff. (*gives him a look, and then turns back to Dick*) I mean, I'm the first to understand that sometimes you have to make some sacrifices to get a good piece of pussy, but don't you think this is a bit too much?

DICK: Guys. Who are you talking to here?

BIFF: Good fucking question.

SLUGGO: Listen, Dick. We're just looking out for you. People have been talking, you know. It doesn't look so good for you to be tying yourself down to one girl. I mean, come on, man, you should be out there slamming as many chicks as possible.

DICK: You're talking to me about slamming chicks? I've slammed more chicks than anyone in this goddamn school.

SLUGGO: That's what I'm saying. Don't you miss it?

DICK: You're talking to me like I'm some old married man.

BIFF: That's the way you're acting.

SLUGGO: What you need to do is come out with us Saturday night. We'll cruise around, pick up some girls. Just like old times.

BIFF (*thrusting his hips back and forth*): Yeah. Bang, bang, bang.

SLUGGO: Easy, Biff.

DICK: Listen, guys. I appreciate your concern. Really. But I've got a good thing going with Jane right now, and I don't want to mess it up.

SLUGGO: Who said anything about messing it up? You can date this chick and still get a little something on the side without her knowing, right? It's not like you've never double-dipped before.

DICK: This is different.

BIFF: Fuck that. I don't care if this girl is the world-champion cocksucker, you don't tie yourself down to one chick when you're still in high school. Do you have any idea how much good pussy there is out there? You know Wilt Chamberlain? You know how many women he fucked? Twenty thousand. Twenty-fucking-thousand.

DICK: Okay, first of all, that's total bullshit. That would be like a different woman every single day for sixty years.

SLUGGO: Or two women a day for thirty years.

BIFF: Or four women a day for fifteen years. Some days he probably banged ten women. The point is, can you imagine if when he was seventeen he had said he was going to stick to one girl and not screw anybody else? Can you even conceive of the amount of pussy he never would have sampled?

SLUGGO: It's a good point, Dick. I mean, if you lined all that pussy up, it would probably stretch from here to China.

BIFF: You ever fucked a Chinese girl, Dick?

DICK: No.

BIFF: Me neither. That's like a whole continent of pussy just waiting for us.

DICK: Dude, you're out of control.

SLUGGO: Hey, I've got a joke. A guy's getting it on with this Chinese chick, and she whispers in his ear, "Tell me what you want." So he says, "I want 69," and she looks all confused, and then says, "You want beef with broccoli?"

DICK (*laughing*): That's horrible, man.

BIFF: Jesus, I'm horny.

DICK: You're always horny.

BIFF: Fuck, yeah.

"Horny"

(Biff, with feeling)
Horny, horny, horny
Starting in the morning
The moment I wake up in my bed
To the bathroom, bolt the lock
Touch my cock, it's like a rock
I want a girl right here to give me head
She's not here, but I don't mope
In the shower with some soap
I give myself some loving instead.

(Sluggo and Biff)
Soapin' up, whackin' off
Whackin' off, soapin' up
Soapin' up, whackin' off
My meat
Whackin' off, soapin' up
Soapin' up, whackin' off
Whackin' off, soapin' up
My meat

(Sluggo, singing directly to Dick)

Ladies, ladies, ladies

I don't want no babies

Just sex without responsibility

A diaphragm or the Pill

Will do the trick, and it will

Let me keep my willy good and free

I hope you don't give me a

Case of gonorrhea

I've already got my share of STDs

(Sluggo and Dick, who gains momentum)

Soapin' up, whackin' off

Whackin' off, soapin' up

Soapin' up, whackin' off

My meat

Whackin' off, soapin' up

Soapin' up, whackin' off

Whackin' off, soapin' up

My meat

(Dick, by now completely swept up

in the playful mood)

Threesome, threesome, threesome

How can I get me some?

Ladies, won't you call up your friends?

All the possibilities

To test our flexibilities

I'd like to see how far your bodies bend

> *The things we will be doing*
> *Like the pornos I've been viewing*
> *(Jane walks onstage. Dick lowers his voice.)*
> *Here comes Jane, and so this song must end.*

DICK: All right, guys. Saturday night. Now get out of here.

SLUGGO: That's what I'm talking about.

(Sluggo and Biff exit. Jane walks over with a puzzled look on her face.)

JANE: What was that all about?

DICK: Nothing. They wanted to know if I had any extra tickets to the opera.

JANE *(laughing)*: I don't know why you still hang out with those guys.

DICK: They're not so bad.

JANE: They're not so good.

DICK *(purposely changing the subject)*: Hey, you want to come over tonight? The house will be empty.

JANE *(smirking)*: To do what?

DICK (*with a devilish smile*): I don't know. Maybe
you can help me with some biology work. (*takes Jane
in his arms*)

JANE (*kissing him*): What exactly are you having
trouble with?

DICK: All this stuff about female anatomy. It's hard
for a guy to keep it all straight.

JANE: Maybe you need some private tutoring.

DICK (*stroking Jane's cheek seductively*): Maybe
I do.

JANE (*smiling*): I think Ms. Bruno has office hours
this afternoon. Why don't you stop by?

DICK: Good idea. A woman in her sixties might be
able to teach me a few things I don't know. I think
she does yoga. Probably very flexible.

JANE (*pulling away*): Okay, that's a picture I don't
need to see.

DICK: You started it.

JANE: I didn't think you were going to turn it into
some sick pornographic fantasy.

DICK: Sorry. So what about tonight?

JANE: I wish I could, but I've got to write a history essay and study for a calculus exam. (*pressing against him*) I'll make it up to you Saturday night.

DICK (*embracing her*): You will, will you? (*They start to kiss, and then Dick abruptly pulls away.*)

JANE: What's wrong?

DICK (*hits his hand to his head*): Oh, no, I totally forgot.

JANE: What?

DICK: I have this family thing on Saturday. Some stupid dinner party at my cousins' house in Marksburg. They do it every year. I don't think I can get out of it.

JANE (*upset*): But we were supposed to go out to dinner to celebrate our one-month anniversary.

DICK: I know. I'd blow off the family thing, but my aunt has cancer, and my mom says this might be the last time she is able to have everybody over. I don't think she's going to make it another year.

JANE: I'm so sorry.

DICK: Yeah, it's tough, especially for her kids. (*shaking his head*) The youngest one's only fourteen. Listen. Why don't we go out Sunday instead?

JANE (*sympathetically*): Sure. You go and be with your family, and don't worry about anything else. (*giving Dick a hug*) You're a good guy, Dick.

DICK: Not really.

(*Jane punches him playfully on the arm and walks off.*)

DICK (*watches her disappear offstage*): I'm going to hell for this one. (*exits*)

(*Curtain*)

CHAPTER EIGHT

"Okay," Maxine said, "who can give me an idea for a protagonist?"

"Bobo the Clown," Bruce called out.

Maxine wrote this on the board. "Okay. What's Bobo's objective?"

"To graduate from clown school," Trish said.

Maxine finished writing this and turned to the class. "What are all the things that are going to make it difficult for Bobo to achieve his objective?"

The answers came fast and furious, and Maxine did not even attempt to write them all down.

"He can't afford the tuition."

"He's not funny."

"Somebody steals his clown shoes."

"He develops a severe allergy to clown makeup."

"A psychopathic clown killer is on the loose and he has to go into hiding."

"He's an alcoholic."

"He's white, and can't get into any clown schools because of affirmative action," Bruce said.

"Okay," Maxine said, cutting off the activity. "You have the idea." She wrote the words STORY ENGINE on the board, and underneath them listed PROTAGONIST, OBJECTIVE, CON-FLICT. "This is what drives your story. One or more main characters trying to achieve specific goals and having to overcome all kinds of challenges along the way."

"Didn't we already go over this?" Bruce asked.

Oh, shut up, Olivia thought.

"We did, but it's important enough to go over again. I want you all to go back to your plays and see if you can map out what your story engines are. I think many of you will find that you need to clarify your characters' objectives and figure out how to increase the amount of conflict."

It was true, Olivia realized as she looked over her work. She had two protagonists, but it wasn't entirely clear what they wanted that they hadn't already found, and to this point there really hadn't been any conflict to speak of. Perhaps now was the moment for things to fall apart and for the story really to kick into gear. Maybe the point was not that they had already gotten together, but whether they would be able to sustain what they had. And so the conflict—which she realized she had already set up—could be that Dick wouldn't be able to keep his dick in his pants, and Jane would become bitter, disillusioned, and hell-bent on castration.

"I'm going to have you pair up today so you can give each other feedback," Maxine said. "I want you to focus first on tightening your story engines, and then you can ask for suggestions on anything you're struggling with." She looked around the room. "Choose someone you haven't worked with yet this summer. It's good to get a fresh set of eyes."

Olivia scanned the room, thinking she might ask Clarissa, a tall, glasses-wearing, slightly bucktoothed girl who always came to class alone and rarely spoke, except in response to someone else. Unfortunately, before Olivia could act on this impulse, Bruce came up and asked if she wanted to be partners with him.

"I was actually about to ask Clarissa," Olivia said.

Bruce looked surprised. "Clarissa?" He turned. "Well, it looks like Trish is asking her."

"Oh, okay," Olivia said, deflating a little.

"So what do you say? You want to go work outside?"

There was no way to say no without seeming like a total bitch.

They found a place on the stairs and Olivia willingly agreed to discuss Bruce's work first. His protagonist was a right-wing conservative college student named George, whose objective was to change the political culture of a radically left-wing university, portrayed as a haven for feminists, Communists, anarchists, and other morally objectionable individuals. The conflict mainly involved George taking on a sadistic, ultraliberal professor with a personal vendetta against him. An additional conflict involved his not getting thrown off-track by the various liberal coeds with whom he became sexually involved. It wasn't terrible, Olivia thought, if only it weren't so disgusting and offensive on so many levels.

Olivia didn't particularly want Bruce reading her script, so she kept the talk around his work going as long as possible. She asked lots of questions and listened to all of his ideas, offered a few suggestions, and prompted him to talk more, which was not so difficult.

"Sorry we didn't get to your play," he said when time was up and they began walking back to class.

"It's okay. I enjoyed just working on yours."

"You're a good partner," he said. "We should work together again."

She didn't answer, and he didn't seem to notice.

When class ended, Trish stayed behind to talk to Maxine, and Olivia began to walk back to the dorm by herself. She had not gone far when suddenly Bruce came up beside her.

"Oh, hi," she said with about as much enthusiasm as someone about to undergo Chinese water torture.

"You going to lunch?" he asked.

Oh God, was he serious? "I'm actually headed back to my dorm first."

"I'll walk with you."

She tried to think of a graceful way to tell him to fuck off. Nothing came to mind. "I can just meet you at the dining hall," she said.

"I don't mind."

This wasn't happening. Why was he stalking her?

They got to the dorm, and he followed her right up the stairs to her suite. Was he for real?

"I'll just run in," she said, preempting him from trying to come inside. She prayed someone was there, so she wouldn't be stuck going to lunch alone with him. Nobody was. Well, as soon as she got to the dining hall, she would take refuge at a table with people she knew.

"Okay," she said, coming back out.

From across the courtyard, Max saw them leaving the dorm together and wondered who Bruce was. He thought about calling out for them to wait, but he needed to take a very large crap before lunch and figured that this wasn't a subject he needed to revisit with Olivia.

The program had movie nights on Fridays, showing films outdoors in the campus courtyard after it got dark. The first two Fridays it had been *Annie Hall* and *North by Northwest.* Tonight it was *The Blues Brothers,* a movie Max had seen many times.

"But have you ever seen it when you were really high?" Zeke asked.

And so before coming out, Max and Zeke got fried out of their minds.

The movie hadn't started yet, but it seemed like everybody in the program was already there, and every patch of grass was occupied by groups of students talking, laughing, and scoping each other out.

"This is crazy," Max said. "Should we go look for Olivia and Trish and those guys?"

"Let's hang back here," Zeke said. "I can't deal with that many people."

"I'm just going to take a loop and see if they're here," Max said. It was a beautiful night, and he was feeling fantastic.

He began to thread through the crowd and realized as he moved farther and farther into the middle of the mass how incredibly stoned he was. What the hell was he thinking? He should have stayed back and met up with them after the movie. He turned around and suddenly began to feel extremely boxed in. Focusing on the ground right in front of him, he pushed forward slowly, careful not to step on anyone, and managed to get himself back to the outside of the crowd. He felt like everyone was looking at him and realizing how fucked up he was. Why the hell had he smoked so much?

He was so caught up in trying to keep from bugging out that at first he didn't fully register the fact that Olivia was standing nearby, scanning the crowd. As he watched her, the boy Max had seen her with earlier that day came up beside her and draped his arm over her shoulders. They talked—Max couldn't hear their words or see Olivia's expression—and then the boy took her hand and led her into the mass of people.

What the fuck? He tried to follow them with his eyes, but he was so thoroughly disoriented that he lost his focus as a group of students walked in front of him, and one of the girls— someone from his acting class—said hi to him.

He had to get out of there before someone tried to have a conversation with him. Staying to the outside and moving straight back away from the screen, he heard the film projector whirl to life, and raucous applause fill the air around him. Where was Zeke? There, sitting in the back of the crowd where he had left him, eyes fixed on the screen, looking completely unperturbed.

"That was a huge mistake," Max said, plopping down next to him.

Zeke smiled. "I told you."

"Your fucking pot," Max said. "You have to remind me."

He tried to concentrate on the movie, but his head was spinning and he couldn't shake the image of Olivia with that boy. He had put his arm around her and then they had been walking together holding hands. Was she going out with him? When the fuck had that happened? What about the fact that Olivia wasn't dating this summer? He tried to see if they were sitting together, but it was too crowded and he was too stoned to be able to distinguish them in the mass. And why would he want to, anyway?

"I'm going to take off," he said.

"Huh?" Zeke said, turning to him. "Where are you going?"

"I just need to get out of here."

He headed out the High Street gate and wandered without direction around downtown New Haven, lost in his own thoughts. The situation with Olivia was making him angrier and angrier. If she was going to hook up with some random boy, then he might as well have fucked Mimi in the bathroom the other night when she threw herself on him. Maybe he still would. Maybe he'd start hooking up with lots of girls. He tried to run through all the possibilities when he suddenly remembered the girl he had met on the train. Hadn't she given him her number? What was her name? He began to scroll through the numbers on his phone. There. Lena Krause. The hot college chick he had flirted with. Should he call her now? He hesitated, wondering if she would even remember him. But then he thought about Olivia with that other boy, and he felt a new wave of anger and sadness wash over him. He had to do something. Taking a deep breath, he dialed, and after several seconds he heard her voice on the other end.

"Hi, Lena?"

"Yeah?"

"This is Max."

Silence.

"We met on the train a couple weeks ago," he added quickly. God, he was more stoned than he had realized.

"Oh, hi," she said enthusiastically.

"So, uh, how's it going?"

"Okay," she said. "What's up?"

"You know. Nothing much." He took another deep breath. "I was just wondering if you, uh, wanted to get together or something."

"Now?" She seemed surprised.

"If you're free."

She did not answer right away, and then she said, "Can you hold on?"

Max waited, his stoned brain turning each second into an eternity.

"I'm supposed to go to a party at my friend's house," she said when she came back on. "Do you want to come?"

"Okay," Max said quickly, feeling a surge of excitement.

"Do you have something to write with? I'll give you the address."

Was he really going to do this? Curfew was in an hour, and you could get in serious trouble if you weren't back in the dorms on time. But fuck it. She was inviting him to a party, and this was not an opportunity he was going to pass up.

"Can you text it to me?" he asked.

Somehow he was able to think clearly enough to realize that if he went back to the dorm and signed in for the night, then maybe he could slip back out and nobody would know he was gone. Granted he would not be able to get back into the dorm until morning, but that was okay. If things worked out the way he hoped they would, he would be out all night anyway.

The only person on the hall when he returned was his resident advisor, who was sitting in his room with the door open, typing on his computer.

"Hey, Shakespeare," Max said, signing the sheet outside his door.

Shakespeare turned in his chair. "I wouldn't come in here if I were you. That pork and beans they served at dinner is wreaking havoc on my bowels."

Max laughed. "Thanks for the warning."

"Were you at the movie?"

"For a little while," Max said. "I've seen it before."

Shakespeare nodded. "I'm actually glad you're here," he said, his voice taking on a more serious tone. "There's something we need to talk about."

"Okay," Max said, tensing slightly. It was hard to get too nervous around someone who shared stories about watching a pornographic movie with his grandmother and who claimed to have once masturbated eleven times in one day. Still, if he knew about the drug use, there could be serious trouble.

"As a fellow Jew, don't you find it a bit problematic that they serve pork on Shabbos?"

Max smiled, relieved that this was just another one of Shakespeare's routines.

"It's downright anti-Semitic," Shakespeare continued. "The next thing you know they'll be forcing us to go to Sunday Mass."

Max shook his head in mock anguish, too stoned to come up with a witty rejoinder on the spot.

"Yellow stars, Max. Mark my words. It's only a matter of time."

"Good night," Max said with a laugh.

"Solidarity, brother," Shakespeare said, thumping his heart with two fingers and then turning back to his computer.

What a freak, Max thought as he walked down the hall. He popped into his room to get a toothbrush and toothpaste, and a few minutes later slipped out of the dorm en route to his rendezvous with blond-haired, blue-eyed Lena Krause.

The movie ended. Olivia grabbed Mimi's hand and said, "Get me upstairs before he comes back." She had managed to dislodge herself from Bruce before the movie started by spotting her suitemates and squeezing into the space they had saved for her.

"I still can't believe he likes you," Trish said.

"If he touches me again, I think I'm going to scream."

They hurried toward the dorm and ran into Zeke by the entryway.

"Hey," Trish said. "Were you at the movie? I was looking around for you."

"I was in the back," he said.

"Where's Max?" Mimi asked.

Zeke shrugged. "He took off when the movie started."

Trish hesitated at the bottom of the stairs. "What are you up to now?"

"I'm kind of tired. I'll see you guys tomorrow." He started down the hall to his room.

As Zeke drifted off to sleep that night, Max was in an apartment across town drinking tequila shots with Lena Krause, and Olivia was sitting at her computer, her mind buzzing with all the different possible paths her story could take.

CASTRATION CELEBRATION

Act 2, scene 3

(*Saturday night, outside Amber's house*)

AMBER: Okay, top ten movie stars you'd want to sleep with.

JANE: I doubt there are ten. Most of them are skeevy.

AMBER: Are you crazy? (*counting on fingers*) Orlando Bloom, Josh Hartnett, Christian Bale, Ryan Phillippe, Jake Gyllenhaal, Will Smith, Viggo Mortensen, Leonardo DiCaprio—

JANE: Leonardo DiCaprio? He looks like a rat.

AMBER: Oh my God, he is so hot. Did you see him at the Oscars?

JANE: Rat Boy. He looks like he's about twelve years old.

AMBER: So who do you like?

JANE: I don't know. Jean Reno, Alan Rickman, Ian McShane.

AMBER: Who?

JANE: Jean Reno. *The Professional*? With Natalie Portman? Anyway, he's been in a million other things. And Alan Rickman. He's gross in *Harry Potter,* but didn't you see *Truly, Madly, Deeply*? Didn't we rent that?

AMBER: The one about the dead guy? That ripped off *Ghost*?

JANE: Ripped off *Ghost*? *Ghost* was filmed after. Anyway, he's directed, too—*The Winter Guest*. Every scene in that film was like an oil painting.

AMBER: Blah, blah, blah. Who's the other guy?

JANE: Ian McShane. From *Deadwood*.

AMBER: The guy who played Sheriff Bullock?

JANE: No, the guy who played Al Swearengen.

AMBER: Are you kidding? He's like fifty years old.

JANE: He's sexy.

AMBER: He's a pimp.

JANE: He's hot. Anyway, I'm really not interested in sleeping with anyone other than Dick.

AMBER: So you guys are sleeping together now? About time.

JANE: What do you mean about time? We've only been dating a month.

AMBER: Is he good in bed?

JANE: None of your business.

AMBER: I guess that means no.

JANE: It means none of your business. (*Amber smiles, and then Jane smiles, too.*) All right, he's fantastic, but it's not like I have much basis for comparison.

AMBER: That's for sure. (*struck by a sudden realization*) Wait. Was this—

JANE (*smiling*): Uh-huh.

AMBER: Oh my God, this is huge! When did it happen?

JANE (*whispering excitedly*): Last weekend. You're the first person I've told. Oh my God, I was so nervous, but Dick was really patient and gentle, and he kept asking me if I was okay. It hurt a little the first time, but we've done it twice since then and it's been amazing.

AMBER (*excited, clapping her hands*): Yayyy! Now come on, let's have the details.

JANE: I just told you.

AMBER: Oh, come on. I want the juicy stuff.

JANE: I'm not going to tell you that.

AMBER: Why not?

JANE: It's private.

AMBER: All right, be that way. But don't expect me to share my sex stories with you anymore.

JANE: Is that a promise?

AMBER: Shut up. You know you love them.

JANE: Not as much as you love telling them.

AMBER: Come on. Please?

(*Jane hesitates.*)

AMBER: Please?

JANE (*smiles and starts to sing*):

"I'm in Love with Dick"

Well, we went back to Dick's room
Last Saturday night
We sat on his bed, we held each other tight
His parents were out late, the whole house was free
I looked at Dick, and Dick looked at me

I saw he was excited, I knew without a doubt
That he would like to love me inside and out
I was feeling nervous, not sure if I should
But something about him made me feel so good

He was really gentle, never pushed too much
Helped me open up, helped me get in touch
With a part of myself I'd always kept suppressed
And now I understand when people
Say that he's the best

Some might call him cocky, he does have a big head
I'd say confident, assertive are better words instead
Before I got to know him, I wondered if we'd click
Now I know for sure that I'm in love with Dick
Yeah, now I know for sure that I'm in love with Dick

AMBER (*laughs*): What have I been telling you?

JANE: I know. You were right.

AMBER: So now that we've gotten you laid, we need to find me a boyfriend.

JANE: My brother's available.

AMBER: I see why you like that guy from *Deadwood*. You're a pimp, too.

(*The girls start to laugh. There is the sound of voices in the distance, and Dick, Sluggo, and Biff appear on the other side of the stage.*)

BIFF: So come on, man, what happened? You were in the bathroom with her forever.

SLUGGO: Please tell me you at least got a blow job.

DICK (*with a little smile*): Whatever. She was drunk. It was no big deal.

SLUGGO (*excitedly*): You're the man. See that, Biff.
First time out in a month and he scores. We go out
every week, and the best I can do is grope some
chick in a crowded bar when she's not looking.

(*They are now within earshot of Jane and Amber but
are too caught up in their conversation to realize
they are not alone.*)

BIFF (*to Dick*): Did you fuck her?

DICK: Nah. I'm not gonna fuck a girl in a dirty
bathroom stall.

BIFF: Yeah, right. (*All three start to laugh.*)

DICK: Listen. I've got a good thing going with Jane,
so this stays with us, you understand.

SLUGGO: Chill, man. It's not like we've never
cheated before.

(*Amber is about to step forward, but Jane holds her
back. She has a dazed and horrified expression.*)

DICK: Okay, then. Remember. I was in Marksburg
tonight at a family reunion, visiting my dying
aunt.

BIFF: Couldn't you come up with something more original? You always use that same story.

DICK: Well, it always works, doesn't it? You got to understand the female psyche. When you talk about going to a family reunion, they think you're going to be a good family man. It's evolutionary. Girls are looking for someone who will be a good husband and a good father. Then when you throw in the shit about a dying relative, they think you're all caring and sensitive and that if they ever get sick you'll spend your every waking hour sitting by their hospital bed.

SLUGGO: Yeah, hitting on the nurses.

DICK: That's what I'm talking about.

JANE (*stepping forward, tears in her eyes*): You filthy piece of shit.

DICK (*startled*): Jane. What are you—

JANE: You filthy, lying sack of shit.

DICK: Jane, calm down. Let me explain.

AMBER (*stepping forward and speaking angrily*): Explain what? We heard the whole conversation.

BIFF: Hey, Amber.

DICK (*approaches Jane*): It's not what you think.

JANE (*hysterical*): Get away from me. Just stay the fuck away. (*She runs off.*)

AMBER: Asshole. (*runs after Jane*)

DICK: FUCK! FUCK, FUCK, FUCK, FUCK, FUCK!!!

SLUGGO: That sucks, man.

BIFF: You see that? That bitch Amber acting like she doesn't even know who I am.

DICK: I've gotta go. (*runs off after Jane and Amber, calling Jane's name*)

(*Curtain*)

CHAPTER NINE

Fate works in mysterious ways, and it was certainly working mysteriously at seven a.m. that Saturday. As Max trudged down Elm Street, eyes on the ground, shoulders sagging, hair uncombed, he heard his name and looked up to see Trish walking toward him. She was wearing biker shorts and a T-shirt and her face was red and she was sweaty and out of breath.

"What are you doing up so early?" she asked as they came together near the campus gate.

Max shrugged and forced a smile. "Just walking."

Trish wiped her face with her sleeve. "Sorry I'm so sweaty. I was jogging." She looked at him more closely and grinned. "You look like you've been out all night."

He hesitated and then looked away. She was staring at him, and he felt a sheepish expression come over his face.

"Oh my God, you were!" she yelped.

Why was she so loud? His head was throbbing, and all he wanted was to get back to his room and go to sleep.

"Where were you? What did you do?"

He was much too tired and hungover to concoct a story, and there was no way he could just make Trish disappear. "I was with a friend," he said. "Listen, I really need to get some sleep."

She walked with him through the gate and across the courtyard, and he silently prayed that she wouldn't ask him any more questions before they got to the dorm.

"So were you with someone from the program?" she asked.

He shook his head. "Just someone I know." He tried to make this mystery person sound like as casual an acquaintance as possible, rather than someone he had been having sex with several hours earlier.

Max eased the room door open and tiptoed toward his bed.

"What time is it?" Zeke asked groggily.

Max turned. "Almost seven-thirty," he whispered. "Sorry if I woke you."

Zeke rubbed his eyes. "Are you just coming in?"

"Yeah." Max sat on his bed, took off his sneakers, and fell back on his pillow. A wave of nausea rippled over him and he felt like he might throw up. "Do you have any Tylenol or anything?"

"I think I have Advil. Check my top drawer."

Max sat up, found the bottle, shook out three tablets, swallowed them without water, and plopped back down. "I feel like shit," he moaned.

"Where were you?" Zeke asked.

"Dude, I had a fucking crazy night."

Zeke waited for him to say more, but he just lay there massaging his temples and staring up at the ceiling.

"What happened?" Zeke asked.

Max allowed a smile to creep over his face. "Fucked a college chick."

Zeke sat up in bed. "Are you serious? Who was she?"

"I met her on the train coming here. She goes to the University of New Haven." He turned over on his side, trying to find any position where his head would stop throbbing and he would not feel so nauseated. "Oh, man, I am so hungover."

"That's why you should stick to pot," Zeke said.

"You're not going to believe this," Trish told her suitemates as they walked to brunch. "This morning, when I was coming back from my jog, I ran into Max, who was just coming in from being out all night."

"No way," Mimi said. "Where was he?"

"I have no idea, but he looked like he was about to pass out."

"Was he by himself?" Olivia asked.

Trish nodded. "He said he had been out with a friend. Someone not in the program."

"I'll bet he was," Callie said, suggestively.

"You think he was with a girl?" Trish asked, surprised.

"Uh, *yeah*," Callie said.

Mimi shook her head. "I don't think so."

"Why not?" Callie asked. "Just because you guys were all over each other the other night?"

"No," Mimi said, offended. "And besides he likes Olivia, not me."

"Whatever," Olivia said, rolling her eyes, but with a sinking feeling that Callie was right.

"Let's bet then," Callie said. "I say Max was out with a girl, and you say he wasn't."

"Okay," Mimi said. "How much?"

Callie shrugged. "Five dollars?"

"Make it more interesting," Olivia said. "How about if Mimi wins, Callie has to make out with a boy, and if Callie wins, Mimi has to make out with a girl?"

"Oh my God!" Mimi squealed. "No way."

"I'm not making out with a boy," Callie said.

"How about just a kiss then?" Olivia persisted. "You both think you're going to win, anyway."

"I don't know," Mimi said. "Maybe we should just bet money."

"Boring," Olivia said, as they walked into the dining hall.

They got their food—rubbery pancakes and lukewarm sausage links for Olivia, Mimi, and Callie, a banana and an apple for Trish—and spotted Zeke sitting by himself.

"No Max," Trish said. "Let's go find out what happened."

They settled in next to him, and he nodded a hello and continued eating.

"So," Trish said, peeling her banana, "is Max still sleeping?"

"Yeah," he grunted, cutting a bite of pancake and sticking it in his mouth.

"You know, I saw him coming in this morning when I was jogging. He said he had been out all night."

Zeke looked up. "You saw him?"

Trish nodded. "He said he had been out with a friend."

Zeke kept his face impassive as he bent back over his plate to impale a piece of sausage on his fork.

The girls watched him and exchanged glances.

"Do you know who he was with?" Trish asked.

He tensed, almost imperceptibly, but still enough for Olivia to notice. "I didn't even know he was staying out last night."

"Was he with a girl?" Callie asked.

"I have no idea." He shoveled the last bites of food in his mouth and stood up.

"Well, what do you think?" Trish pushed.

"Why don't you ask him?" Zeke said. He started away from the table, then turned and faced Olivia. "I finished that song you gave me."

"Really?" she said. "Can we get together later so I can hear it?"

"Just come find me," he said, turning and walking off.

Max stood in the shower, letting the hot water wash over him. He had woken up in the middle of the afternoon, feeling dirty and disoriented. His head still hurt. His eyes were bloodshot. He was hungry, but the thought of putting food in his mouth was making him feel slightly queasy.

As he replayed the events of the previous night in his head, the evening took on a surreal quality. He knew he had slept with Lena, could summon the exact images, but somehow, it didn't feel real. They had left the party and gone back to her apartment. She had thrown up. And then, while she was brushing her teeth, he had massaged her neck and back and pressed into her from behind. He felt himself starting to get hard as he remembered, and quickly soaped up his hands.

A little later, dried off and dressed, he called his friend Andy back home to tell him about his night. When he got voicemail, he left a quick message to call and went to e-mail him.

Upstairs, Olivia was staring at a blank computer screen, trying to figure out how to start the third act of her play. She had been sitting there for the past two hours, occasionally writing a few lines, and then reading them over and deleting them. Her frustration mounting, she had even called home, deciding to preempt the Saturday call that would come later in the day from her mother anyway. The problem, she was starting to realize, was that she was preoccupied with trying to figure out what Max had done all night and who this mystery person he was with could be. Somehow, not knowing was blocking her from being able to continue her play. If she could just find out, she was convinced she would be able to move forward. Clicking onto instant messaging, she saw that he was online, and she quickly typed:

> **Olivia123:** Heard you had a wild night
> last night.

Sitting at his computer, Max was surprised to see her message pop up. How did she know? He had told Trish he had stayed out, but only Zeke knew what had happened. And why would Olivia even care considering the fact that she had blown him off for some other guy? He typed:

Maxmania: Looked like you were having a pretty good night yourself.

Olivia123: What do you mean?

Maxmania: Who's the boy?

Olivia123: What are you talking about?

Maxmania: Walking out of the dorm with you yesterday . . . holding hands at the movie . . . so much for being off boys this summer.

Olivia123: Bruce? Are you mental? He's been stalking me.

Maxmania: You didn't seem to mind last night.

Olivia123: All right, Sherlock, you caught me. Bruce is my secret lover and we've been having wild sex all over campus this summer.

Maxmania: I knew it. Details, please, and don't leave anything out.

Olivia123: You first. What does a high school boy do all night in New Haven?

Maxmania: Come downstairs to my room, and I'll show you.

Olivia123: I thought goats weren't allowed in the dorms.

Maxmania: I'm not much for following rules. You know, the penis has a mind of its own.

Olivia123: Very profound. Can I use that in my play?

Maxmania: As long as I get credit for it.

Olivia123: I'll include you in my acknowledgments.

Olivia clicked off IM, opened a new Word document, and typed *THE PENIS HAS A MIND OF ITS OWN* over and over again until she had filled one page and jumped onto the next. Maxine had suggested free writing as a way to break through writer's block. Just spew out whatever comes to mind, she had said. Olivia stopped, took a breath, and started to write again.

The penis has a mind of its own. Is this true? Do guys really want to sleep with as many people as possible? Wilt Chamberlain says he slept with twenty thousand women. Would every guy do it if he could? So why do guys even go through the charade of committing themselves to one person if all they want to do is fuck anything with breasts? And what about gay guys? Are they just as horny? Is a whole guy's life just one big struggle between what he wants and what society says is okay? Id versus ego or superego or whatever Freud said. Penis versus conscience.

A test of testosterone.

Caught between a cock and a hard place.

So is the brain the master of the penis or is the penis the master of the brain? For thousands of years, philosophers have pondered this question. Which came first, the chicken or the egg? Which came first, the penis or the brain? Brains don't come, only penises do. Why did the penis cross the road? To come somewhere else. How many penises does it take to screw in a lightbulb? How can you screw in a lightbulb? Why do guys name their penises?

Penis

Dick

Cock

Willy

Free Willy

Willy Wonka

King Dong

The Sperminator

How many words can you make out of penis?

Snip

snipe

nip

pin

sin

pen

is

The pen is mightier than the sword.
The penis mightier than the sword.
All hail King Cock.

Mimi came into the room and saw Olivia sitting at her computer. "How's the writing coming?" she asked.

"It's coming," Olivia said, suppressing a smile. "It was hard for a while, but I just got one big spurt."

"I love when that happens," Mimi said, and Olivia burst into laughter.

"What? What's so funny?" She looked at Olivia's computer screen. "Oh, gross," she said.

Olivia laughed harder, and Mimi joined in.

"What are you two doing in here?" said Callie, appearing in the doorway. "Having another orgy?"

"Olivia's being perverted again," Mimi said through suppressed giggles.

Olivia recovered her composure and feigned innocence. "Come on, me?"

"Come on you?" Callie said.

Olivia laughed. "You'd like that, wouldn't you?"

"Ewww," Mimi said, scrunching up her face.

"Oh, by the way," Olivia said. "I think Callie won the bet about who Max was with last night."

"Wait, how do you know?" Mimi asked.

"I was IMing with him before, and I asked him what he did last night, and he said to come down to his room and he'd show me."

"Boys are pigs," Callie said, shaking her head.

"That doesn't prove anything," Mimi said, though with a decided lack of conviction.

"Well, get this," Olivia continued. "He thought *I* was with Bruce."

"Stalker Boy?" Mimi asked incredulously.

Olivia nodded. "I guess he saw when Bruce grabbed my hand at the movie and thought we were together. Pretty stupid, right?"

"And you wonder why I'm a lesbian," Callie said.

"I still don't see what any of this proves," Mimi said. "Just because he thought you were with Bruce doesn't mean he went out and hooked up with another girl."

"You want to double the bet?" Callie asked.

Mimi hesitated. "No."

"When did you realize you liked girls?" Olivia asked.

Callie smiled. "You thinking about changing sides?"

"Maybe."

She came in and sat down on Olivia's bed. "You want the short version or the long one?"

"The long one," Olivia said, winking at Mimi. "And don't leave anything out."

"I was in tenth grade," Callie said. "I had this friend Lane, and we spent most of our time criticizing everyone else in the class behind their backs. We both knew we didn't fit in, but I never really wanted to admit why I was so unhappy. I had known for a while that I was attracted to girls, but I didn't know any lesbians. I was living in the South, in the suburbs, where you didn't just go around announcing you were gay unless you were some kind of sadist. So one time I was over at Lane's house, and we're sitting on her bed looking at some magazine or something, and all of a sudden she just leans over and kisses me. I'm totally shocked, but I don't say anything and I start kissing her back. And then we just go crazy, because we've both got all this pent-up sexual energy. It was unbelievable."

"So what happened?" Olivia asked.

Callie shook her head. "After a few weeks, Lane dumped me for Mark Praeger, the quarterback on the football team."

"Oh my God," Mimi said. "That's so sad."

"It was worse for Lane. He ended up giving her herpes."

Olivia laughed.

"Are you serious?" Mimi asked, wide-eyed.

Callie smiled. "No, but it would have served her right." She got up from the bed. "Anyway, if things hadn't ended with Lane, I wouldn't have become obsessed with Brooke and signed up for the drama club and realized how much I liked acting and ended up here this summer."

"So did you and Brooke start dating?" Olivia asked.

Callie shook her head and started toward the door. "I don't even know for sure if she's gay."

"You never asked her?"

"It's not the kind of thing you ask your teacher." She raised her hand in farewell. "I'll see you guys later."

"I love her," Olivia said when Callie had left.

"Oh my God, totally," Mimi said. She popped up and began examining herself in the mirror. "So what about Max?"

"What about him?"

"He really likes you."

Olivia shook her head and chuckled. "He likes anything with breasts."

"That's not true," Mimi said, turning to face her roommate. "He didn't kiss me when he had the chance."

"He didn't push you away, either." She came over and stood next to Mimi. "I'm telling you, between Max and Bruce, I think I might just hide out in my room for the rest of the summer."

"They'll come looking for you, you know."

Olivia thought for a moment. "Well, just tell them that I have a rare infectious disease and if they come too close their penises will fall off."

Mimi laughed. "What about going to class?"

"Trish can fill me in on what I miss. And you guys can all sneak food for me from the dining hall."

"You're crazy," Mimi said.

"Good. Every great writer is a little bit crazy." She walked across the room, sat at her computer, opened to a blank page, and began to type.

"You're not really going to skip dinner, are you?" Mimi asked.

"Yep," Olivia said, not looking away from her screen.

Mimi watched her, waiting for her to say something else, but Olivia continued to type without turning or speaking.

"So you want me to bring something back?" Mimi asked at last.

"That would be great."

"What do you want?"

"Whatever. Just a sandwich would be good. And maybe a can of pepper spray."

Mimi left, chuckling, and Olivia continued to type without looking up.

CASTRATION CELEBRATION

Act 3, scene 1

(*Two days later. Jane, dressed all in black, sits
on her bed reading* The Bell Jar *by Sylvia Plath.
Amber knocks on the door. Jane ignores the knock
and keeps reading. Amber knocks again, and again
Jane continues to read without looking up.*)

AMBER: I know you're in there, Jane.

(*Jane does not look up or respond.*)

AMBER: I brought cookies. Homemade chocolate chip.

(*Jane does not look up or respond.*)

AMBER: You can't stay in there forever, and I'm not
leaving until you let me in.

(*Jane does not look up or respond. Amber begins to
sing "Row, Row, Row Your Boat" very loudly. After
several rounds, Jane puts down her book with an
exasperated look, walks to the door, opens it, then
returns to her bed and resumes reading.*)

AMBER: Jesus, it's like a sauna in here. Let me open
up a window and get some air circulation. (*Opens
window. Jane continues to ignore her. Amber sits*

down on the bed and looks at what Jane is reading.)
Sylvia Plath, huh? Didn't she, like, kill herself?

JANE (*without looking up*): Yes.

(*long pause*)

AMBER: How'd she do it?

JANE: Cooking gas.

AMBER: Not very original.

(*Jane does not respond. The silence hangs heavy.*)

AMBER: So what is this? You're going to spend the
rest of your life shut up in your room reading books
about death?

JANE: Do you have a better idea?

AMBER: What about school?

JANE: What about it?

AMBER: You can't stay out forever.

(*Jane goes back to reading her book.*)

AMBER: Well, Dick was looking for you today. He's going crazy trying to talk to you. He said he's left you like fifty messages on your cell phone. (*Amber waits for Jane to respond. Long silence as Jane continues to read her book.*) You'd think after a while he would realize you don't want to talk to him.

(*Jane continues to read her book.*)

AMBER: He gave me a note to give to you. Do you want it?

(*Jane reaches out, takes the note, and rips it into pieces without reading it. Then she returns to her book.*)

AMBER: Oh, don't be so melodramatic. You're upset. Dick cheated on you. You should be upset. But come on. Guys cheat on their girlfriends all the time. My dad's cheated on my mom more times than I can count. (*pause*) Look. I know this probably doesn't make you feel better, but it's just a fact of life. Even guys with good intentions end up screwing around. The penis has a mind of its own.

JANE (*putting down her book*): That's your theory? That guys have no control over their penises?

AMBER: Pretty much.

JANE (*angrily*): Bullshit. There are plenty of guys out there who don't cheat on their girlfriends.

AMBER: But they all want to. Some just have more self-control.

JANE: That's so depressing.

AMBER: I know.

(*long pause*)

JANE: I wish I were a lesbian.

AMBER (*laughing*): It's never too late to change.

JANE: Have you ever tried it?

AMBER: What? Being a lesbian? No.

JANE: You've never kissed a girl?

AMBER: Why, have you?

JANE: When I was little. My friend Sally and I would pretend to get married. We would have a wedding ceremony and at the end we would kiss each other.

AMBER: Any tongue?

JANE: Gross. We were in first grade.

AMBER: You know, there is a lesbian club at school. Lola Crest started it last year, and they're always looking for new members. She's tried to get me to come a couple of times.

JANE: I don't think so. .

AMBER: Why not?

JANE: I'm not a lesbian.

AMBER: But you want to be. You just said so.

JANE: I was kidding.

AMBER: Well, I doubt you have to be a lesbian to join. It's probably enough if you hate men.

JANE: Do lesbians hate men?

AMBER: Well, they hate penises.

JANE: I should have known better than to date a guy named Dick.

(*There is a knock on the door.*)

JANE: Who is it?

SAM: It's me.

AMBER: Wait. Don't come in. I'm in my underwear.

JANE (*quietly to Amber*): You're horrible. (*loudly*) It's fine, Sam. You can come in.

(*Sam enters awkwardly, stealing a glance at Amber and blushing deeply.*)

SAM: Mom wanted to know if you would be coming down for dinner tonight.

JANE: What are we having?

SAM: Spaghetti and meatballs, I think.

AMBER: Meatballs. Yum.

SAM: You can stay. I mean, I'm sure it's fine if you want to have dinner here.

AMBER (*smiling*): Only if I get to sit next to you.

SAM (*blushing*): Okay.

JANE: Tell Mom we'll be down when dinner is ready.

(*Sam nods, steals a final glance at Amber, and walks out.*)

JANE: You have to stop tormenting him.

AMBER: I'll tell you, Jane, if he was a couple years older—

JANE: How do we keep him sweet and innocent? I don't want my brother turning into a typical teenage guy.

AMBER: Nothing you can do, sweetie. And let me tell you, he's going to be a heartbreaker.

JANE (*shaking her head resignedly*): Fuck me.

AMBER: See. Maybe you are a lesbian.

(*Curtain*)

CHAPTER TEN

"Olivia's really boycotting the dining hall?" Max asked when she did not appear for a second day in a row.

"Not the dining hall," Callie said. "Just you."

Trish laughed, and Mimi gave Callie a disapproving glance. "Don't be so mean," she said.

Callie shrugged. "It's true."

"Wait," Max said. "You're saying she's not coming because of me?"

"Pretty much," Callie said, nodding.

"She's just totally focused on her musical right now," Mimi said gently. "I'm sure she'll be back soon."

"Did I do something to piss her off?" he asked.

"I don't know," Callie said, raising her eyebrows. "Did you?"

"Not that I know of," Max said, willing himself to keep a straight face even though the implication of Callie's question was clear. "She was IMing with me yesterday, and she didn't say anything."

"If you say so," Callie said with a sarcastic edge.

Max looked down at his plate, pushed his food around a bit, and then absently took a bite of spaghetti.

"This is stupid," Mimi said, turning to Max. "You like her, right?"

"What difference does it make?"

"You have to show her," Mimi said.

Max shook his head. "What's the point? She's already said she's not interested."

"Then make her interested," Mimi said earnestly.

"Sure," he said, nodding at each of the girls before returning his attention to Mimi. "I mean, she's only turned me down once this summer, and decided that she'd rather starve to death than sit through a meal with me, so it shouldn't be too hard to convince her."

"Speaking of starving to death," Callie said, looking meaningfully at Trish.

"I'm eating," Trish said, holding up her apple. She took a bite and turned to Max. "Where's Zeke tonight?"

Max took a sip of juice. "He said he didn't feel like eating."

"Is he okay?"

He shrugged. "I think he's dealing with stuff back home. Do you know his friend Devin?"

"Kind of," Trish said, frowning slightly. "They used to be in a band together."

Max took a bite of his buttered roll and chewed without tasting. How could Olivia dislike him so much that she didn't even want to see him anymore? That was it? She was just going to cut the strings and walk away? There was no way he could deal with that. There was just no way.

"Is Olivia back at the dorm now?" he asked.

Mimi nodded and smiled.

He looked at the food on his tray and realized he had no interest in eating any of it. "Maybe I should go talk to her," he said.

"You should," Mimi said encouragingly.

Callie shook her head. "It's your funeral."

When Max knocked, Olivia was writing about lesbians. She went to the door and, after hearing Max identify himself, rolled her eyes and let him in.

"I brought you a brownie," he said, handing over a lumpy napkin.

"That's so sweet," she said, extracting the brownie and taking a bite. "Come on in."

He sat on one couch and she sat on the other, and he looked at her in her sweats and T-shirt, looked at her red hair and her freckled face, looked as she took another bite of her brownie and caught the crumbs in her hand, and he felt something stir inside him.

"Why are you looking at me like that?" she asked, wiping around her mouth with the napkin. "Do I have chocolate on my face?"

"No," he said, smiling and shaking his head.

When she finished her brownie, she got up to throw her napkin away and to steal a glance in the mirror to make sure her face really was clean.

"Did you see Mimi, Trish, and Callie in the dining hall?" she asked, sitting back down.

"Yeah, they're still eating."

"So did they tell you why I haven't been there?" she asked.

He hesitated. "Callie said you're avoiding me." He tried to keep his voice light.

"Not just you. Boys in general."

"Oh," he said. "A boy boycott."

"Pretty much," she laughed.

"What about Bruce, or whatever his name is?"

"I can't believe you thought I liked him," she said.

Max held open his hands. "I'm sorry. It looked like you guys were together."

"Yuck," she said, screwing up her face. "Do you know what I did after class today?"

"What?"

"I told him I was a lesbian."

Max laughed. "Did he believe you?"

"Who knows?" she said with a shrug. "At least he didn't try to follow me back to the dorm again."

Max readjusted himself on the couch. "So this boycott," he said, pausing. "Is there any room for negotiation?"

She chuckled and shook her head. "I don't think so."

"Really? There's nothing I could do to make you reconsider?"

"No," she said. "Not unless you're willing to consider castration."

He raised his eyebrows. "That's a pretty steep asking price."

"Those are my terms," she said with a shrug.

He cupped his chin and nodded slowly, making little noises of deep contemplation. "Just to be clear," he asked after a moment. "You'd only take the testicles, right, not the whole kit and caboodle?"

"Just the testicles," she said impassively.

But before he could respond, voices rang through the hall outside and then a loud knock resonated through the room. "Is it safe to come in?" Mimi called.

"Hurry," Max yelled. "She's got a knife."

"I knew it," Callie's voice boomed. The door flew open, and Max and Olivia smiled from the couches.

"She was threatening to castrate me," Max said.

Olivia got up and shook her head. "I'm going back to work. Thanks for the brownie, Max."

He didn't stay long after that. When he got back to his room, Zeke was gone, but the familiar smell of marijuana permeated the air. He found a piece of paper, sat down, and began to write.

> Dear Olivia,
>
> After long and hard deliberation, I've come to the conclusion that your terms are just too stiff, and it would be nuts for me to play ball under such hairy conditions. But I'm willing to do almost anything else you ask. Please don't cut off negotiations.
>
> Eagerly awaiting your reply,
> Max

He ran upstairs and slid the note under the girls' door, figuring that even if Olivia wasn't interested, it would be almost impossible for the group of them to resist his offer.

And he was correct. A little more than an hour later, the response arrived. It read:

Dear Max,

Upon the recommendation of my advisers, I have modified my demands. If you wish me to end my boycott, then here is what you have to do:

At dinner tomorrow night, at precisely six-thirty, get everybody's attention in the dining hall and perform an original monologue about your decision to be castrated.

Get Callie to kiss you.

If, and only if, you have completed the two tasks above, submit to an interview in front of a panel of my choosing, after which the panel members will decide, by simple majority vote, whether or not I should go out with you.

This offer is final.

Sincerely,

Olivia

Max smiled as he read Olivia's note, then scribbled his reply and slipped it under her door.

Dear Olivia,

You're sick, but I accept your challenge. Let the games begin.

The first part of the test was the easiest. He was an actor, he had written and performed monologues before, and he loved the spotlight. The fact that his subject was castration did not daunt him in the least. He just needed to be sure to get it written and memorized quickly to make Olivia's cutoff.

It was amazing how many sites came up when he Googled castration. Well over three million. He scrolled through: Is Castration Right for Me? Castration Blogs, Photos, and Videos. Police Investigate Botched Castration. Dog Castration. Chemical Castration Bill Becomes Law. Thankfully, this last one was satirical.

He heard the door open and looked up from his computer to see Zeke walking in. "Hey," Max said.

Zeke walked over to his bed, sat down, and began to unlace his sneakers. "What's up?"

"Listen to this," Max said, turning back to the computer screen. "In Europe, they used to castrate boys to keep their voices from changing at puberty, because girls weren't allowed to sing in church choirs."

"What the hell site are you on?"

"I'm doing research on castration," Max said.

"Well, I don't need to hear that shit. It's bad enough I have to go to church on Christmas and Easter." Zeke finished taking off his sneakers and carried them to the closet.

Max couldn't tell what kind of mood Zeke was in, but decided it was safest to keep things light. "You ever been molested by a priest?" he asked.

"Ever had your penis sliced by a rabbi?" Zeke shot back.

Max laughed. "It's called a *mohel*. But that gives me a good idea." He clicked open a Word document.

"I'm going to take a shower," Zeke said, grabbing his towel and walking out.

Max began to type and found that the words came easily. Almost too easily. He wondered what his therapist might have to say about that. Just before midnight, he put his computer to sleep, and after class the next day he put the finishing touches on his work, read it aloud, and made a few revisions. Before dinner, he practiced performing for Zeke, who told him that he was seriously disturbed. At six-thirty he stood on his chair in the dining hall, and the girls at his table banged their spoons against their glasses. "If I can have everybody's attention," he called out in a booming voice, "I will now perform an original monologue about castration."

There was widespread laughter and a few shouted comments and then the room quieted, and he began.

"I know you don't think it's a good idea, Mom, but will you please just listen. You're not a guy, so you have no way of knowing how hard it is to have testosterone coursing through your veins. I walk around every day with this beast in my pants screaming 'FEED ME! FEED ME!' You're laughing, but it's really not funny. Remember when I was a baby, and I would throw a tantrum if you didn't play with me. It's like that. If I don't attend to HIM constantly, there's no telling what might happen. I could be standing in front of the class doing a presentation, and suddenly Bilbo Baggins decides it's time for a growth spurt. Not cool, Mom. Not cool. Why do you think I spend so much time in the bathroom? Do you think I volunteer to wash my own sheets out of the goodness of my heart? I'm sorry if that grosses you out, but it's true. And come on, don't act like removing the testicles is such a big deal. I mean, you sliced off part of my penis when I was eight days old and threw a party to celebrate.

"Look, this isn't just one of my crazy ideas, like wanting to go to mime school or going on that all-bread diet. This time, I've done the research and know it's really what I want. I've been on-line talking to eunuchs from all over the country. Have you ever even met a eunuch, Mom? Well, you should. They're some of the smartest, funniest, most successful people I've ever talked to. And you know what they all say? That they're much happier now that they've got their sex drives under control.

"I've made up my mind, Mom, and you can't stop me. I've made an appointment to have it done on Friday after school. (*pause*) I know it's Shabbos, Mom, but it was the only day he had open. (*pause*) His name is Doctor Denutter, and yes, he's fully licensed. (*pause*) What kind of question is that? I have no idea what he does with them afterward. (*pause*) Are you serious? What would you do with them? (*pause*) You want to keep them as a souvenir? What the hell's the matter with you? (*pause*) I can't have this conversation right now, Mom. I can't . . . (*looks down*) Oh, Jesus, no! Not now! Down, boy, down! (*to Mom*) See. I told you it was out of control. I've got to go."

Max sat down to a round of hearty applause, though a number of boys in the room wore horrified expressions and had positioned their hands protectively over their crotches. He caught Olivia's eye and winked. She gave him a little smile, then pointed at Callie, who was sitting across the table, brandishing her knife and fork.

That's right. Now he had to get Callie to kiss him. Things were about to get a lot more interesting.

CASTRATION CELEBRATION
Act 3, scene 2

(A classroom. Jane and three other girls sit in chairs facing a fifth girl, who is standing at the front of the room.)

LOLA: The meeting will come to order. Before we get started, let's welcome Jane, who is joining us for the first time. (There are smiles, nods, and light applause from the other girls.) Okay. The first item on today's agenda is Outrage of the Week. What we do, Jane, is share the most outrageous forms of harassment and discrimination we have experienced or witnessed over the past week. Who wants to share first?

CAROL: I will. I read in the newspaper this week that the school board is trying to ban a book about gay monkeys from school libraries.

JESSE: Oh my God, I saw that, too. What the fuck is wrong with these people? It's okay to have books

158

about guns, but you can't have a book about gay monkeys?

KITTY: There are gay monkeys? That's so cool.

CAROL: Of course there are gay monkeys. There are gay monkeys, gay gorillas, gay giraffes, gay penguins, gay aardvarks. You think only people can be gay?

KITTY: Wow! I never thought about that before. Do you think there were gay dinosaurs?

JESSE: Have you seen Barney?

CAROL: Hey, what about this for a TV show? A sitcom where all the characters are talking dinosaurs, and the main character is gay.

JESSE: Penisaurus Rex.

CAROL: Cunnilingusaurus.

KITTY: Is Barney really gay?

LOLA: We're getting off topic. Does anyone else have an outrage to share?

JESSE: I do.

KITTY (*to Jane*): Jesse always has an outrage.

JESSE: Jane was there for this one.

JANE: Gym class?

JESSE: Uh-huh. Yesterday, in gym, Mr. Grunfeld divided the class into girls and boys, and that cunt Christie Meehan says, "Can Jesse go on the boys' side? I don't want her trying to rape me." Can you believe that shit? And everyone laughs, including fucking dickhead Grunfeld.

CAROL: What did you do?

JESSE: I looked at Christie and said, "Why don't you go? You've already slept with all of them anyway."

CAROL (*laughing*): You said that? Oh my God.

KITTY: What happened?

JESSE: Grunfeld made meowing noises, so I gave him the finger and walked out of class.

KITTY: You did not.

JESSE: Ask Jane.

KITTY (*turning to Jane*): Did she really?

JANE: She did. But he deserved it.

LOLA: You won't get in trouble. That asshole's hanging on to his job by a thread, and everyone knows it.

KITTY: Didn't he make a pass at a student a few years ago?

LOLA: Are you kidding? He hits on his students all the time. I heard he slept with Jordan Weston's sister when she was a senior.

CAROL: Yuck! He's so slimy!

JANE: All guys are slimy!

JESSE (*looking at Jane with approval*): You said it, sister.

KITTY (*confused*): Wait. You hate guys? I thought you were going out with Dick Conroy.

JANE: I was. I'm not anymore.

JESSE: It's a good thing, or we might have to beat some sense into you.

JANE: I wish someone had beat some sense into me before I went out with him.

CAROL: What happened?

JANE: I really don't want to talk about it.

LOLA: Come on, Jane. This is a support group. You'll feel better getting it all out.

JANE: There's nothing really to tell. He lied to me and screwed around behind my back.

JESSE: Of course he did. Men are scum.

LOLA: Tell us what happened.

JANE (*uncertainly*): Well, we had been going out for a month. We were supposed to go out to dinner to celebrate our anniversary.

JESSE: I'm gonna puke.

LOLA: Jesse! Go ahead, Jane.

JANE: Well, he tells me he has to go to a family reunion to see his dying aunt. But instead he goes out with his friends and hooks up with some random drunk girl in a bathroom stall.

CAROL: What a pig!

LOLA: I'm so sorry, Jane.

JESSE: All men should be castrated!

CAROL: That's Jesse's answer for everything.

JESSE: Tell me the world wouldn't be a better place with no penises.

KITTY: You can't just go around castrating people, Jesse.

JESSE: It's ridiculous that men have more power than women when everyone knows that women are the dominant sex. (*She takes a paper out of her bag and begins to read.*) "The male is a biological accident: the Y (male) gene is an incomplete X (female) gene, that is, has an incomplete set of chromosomes. In other words, the male is an incomplete female, a walking abortion, aborted at the gene stage. To be male is to be deficient, emotionally limited; maleness is a deficiency disease and males are emotional cripples."

JANE (*laughing*): What is that?

JESSE: SCUM Manifesto.

KITTY: SCUM?

JESSE: Society for Cutting Up Men. Some chick wrote this back in the sixties.

JANE: Smart lady.

JESSE: I know, right? Listen to this. (*starts to read again*) "Life in this society being, at best, an utter bore and no aspect of society being at all relevant to women, there remains to civic-minded, responsible, thrill-seeking females only to overthrow the government, eliminate the money system, institute complete automation, and destroy the male sex."

LOLA: Ladies, take up arms!

CAROL: Down with men!

JESSE: A castration celebration!

(*Music begins*)

"Castration Celebration"

(*Lola*)

There's a land that I see where the women are free
It's a land full of joys,
Where we rule the men and boys

Take my hand, come with me,

Oh how happy we will be

Come with me, take my hand, and we'll live

In a land where the men do the chores

(Kitty)

In a land with no macho guy wars

(Jesse)

In a land where we're more than just whores

(all together)

Cuz we don't need men to succeed anymore

(Jane)

I look ahead to a nation

Where we've stripped away temptation

Don't depend on the men;

You don't need the aggravation

So be strong, keep your heart . . .

From being torn apart

Keep your heart, and be strong, join the fight

(Lola)

For a land where the men do the chores

(Kitty)

For a land with no macho guy wars

(Jesse)

For a land where we're more than just whores

(Carol)

For a land with no Hooters or Scores

(all together)

Cuz we don't need men to succeed anymore

(Jesse)

Every boy in this nation

Is subject to castration

Every girl in this world

Can join the celebration

Take a knife, drop the mop,

All it takes is just one chop

Drop the mop, take a knife, and we'll run

(Lola)

To a land where men do the chores

(Kitty)

To a land with no macho guy wars

(Jesse)

To a land where we're more than just whores

(Carol)

To a land with no Hooters or Scores

(Jane)

To a land where a woman can roar

(all together)

> That we don't need men to succeed
>
> No, we don't need men to succeed
>
> No, we don't need men to succeed anymore.

JESSE (still swept up in the spirit of the song):
Let's go trash the boys' locker room.

(The other girls give each other uncomfortable looks.)

KITTY: Um. I've kind of got a lot of homework.

CAROL: Yeah, I have an English paper due Friday on
Moby-Dick.

(Jesse turns to Jane.)

JANE: Don't look at me. I'm only a lesbian wannabe.

LOLA: Maybe we can put it on the agenda for next week.

JESSE (disgustedly): So much for the revolution.

(Dick appears onstage, looking around. He walks
into the classroom.)

DICK: Jane. There you are. (sees the other girls and
registers that this is a meeting of the Lesbian
Club) What are you doing here?

JESSE (*wrapping her arm protectively around Jane*): She's one of us now. You got a problem with that?

DICK (*ignoring Jesse*): Can we talk? Alone?

JANE: There's nothing to talk about.

(*Dick looks at the other girls, who all glare at him.*)

DICK (*to Jane*): Come on, Jane. This is ridiculous. Let me walk you home.

JESSE (*looks at Jane*): Is he really as dumb as he seems?

JANE: Uh-huh.

DICK (*chuckling*): Fine. (*He looks at the girls.*) Ladies, have a nice afternoon. (*to Jane*) I'll call you later.

JANE: Don't bother.

(*Dick gives her one last look and exits. There is a moment of silence and then the girls start to laugh and whoop it up.*)

(*Curtain*)

CHAPTER ELEVEN

Callie did not consider herself a cruel person. She volunteered at the local soup kitchen. She defended an overweight classmate from the mean girls in eighth grade. She cried when she saw *To Kill a Mockingbird*. She never tortured substitute teachers and only tortured her incredibly annoying younger brother on rare occasions. Still, the potential for messing with Max's mind was too tempting to resist.

It started in acting class the day after his castration monologue. He approached her and asked if she wanted to partner up that day. It was all so obvious. They were doing improvisation activities and he would try to steer their scene toward a kiss.

"Ten dollars," she said.

"What do you mean ten dollars?"

"I'll be your partner for ten dollars."

He considered this, trying to figure out if she was serious. "How about five?"

"No, thanks," she said, shaking her head and immediately joining up with another boy in the class.

He stepped up his campaign the next day, no longer even trying to hide his true intentions. "I'll give you twenty dollars if you kiss me," he said.

"Do I look like a whore?" she said in mock indignation.

"Okay, fifty dollars."

She stared at him in disbelief. "Let's see it."

He pulled out his wallet, extracted two twenties and a ten, and held the bills out to her.

"Here's the thing," she said, keeping her arms folded. "I really don't need the money, and the thought of kissing a boy makes me feel like I might vomit."

"Then just close your eyes and pretend I'm a girl," Max said.

Callie shook her head. "It won't work."

"Well, how about if I put on a wig?"

"Forget it," she said, turning away. She took a few steps, then suddenly turned back. "I'll tell you what," she said. "If you completely make yourself over as a girl, and I think you're hot enough, I'll consider it."

Max laughed. "Seriously?"

"Sure," she said with a shrug. "But I should warn you I'm very picky."

"So what's your type?" he asked.

She smiled devilishly and walked away.

Max could barely contain his excitement at the prospect of making himself over. The year before he had dressed up as a girl on Halloween and paraded through the French Quarter, drawing admiring hoots and whistles from other revelers on Bourbon Street. Of course then he had just tried to make himself look as slutty as possible for a crowd that was more drunk than sober; but for Callie, who did not merely see girls as sex objects, he knew he would need a more sophisticated look.

He lingered after class to speak to his teacher. He had a strange question, he said. Was there someone in the program who could make him look like a girl?

Mr. Wells was curious. Was this for an acting role, or were there other, deeper identity issues that Max was struggling with? Not that it mattered to him. He just needed to know whether to recommend a makeup artist or a psychiatrist.

Max smiled and assured Mr. Wells that it was all in good fun, and Mr. Wells suggested he ask the girls in the class for advice. "Perhaps Mimi," he said with a glint in his eye. "I imagine she would be amenable to this sort of endeavor."

"Oh my God," she squealed when Max pulled her aside after lunch and asked her. "It will be so much fun. We can go shopping right now."

And Mimi, of course, was a genius. They bought a simple linen dress at J. Crew and a bra at Urban Outfitters, and Mimi booked appointments for him to get his hair and nails done the next day. Throughout it all, Max was gracious and charming. He knew that if he could pull this off, he would be one step closer to Olivia, and he was willing to do anything to get there. But beyond that, he was having fun. A head massage with his blowout? A pedicure—now he knew why girls loved them—with foot massage, a vibrating chair, and hot towels? It was good to be a girl, he thought. Expensive, yes, but very good.

That night in his room, Mimi did his makeup and, after finishing with a bit of lipstick, stood back to admire her handiwork. "Oh my God," she said. "You look amazing. Don't you think, Zeke?"

"I'd do him," Zeke said.

Max looked in the mirror and smiled. He looked good, no question about it. Better than most of the girls in the program. He adjusted his breasts and hoped he wouldn't get hard just staring at himself.

"Ready?" Mimi asked.

Callie had insisted that Max unveil himself in the girls' suite in front of the whole gang.

"I'll run up and tell them you're coming," she said. "You guys come up in two minutes."

He paced around the room, and then stood looking at himself in the mirror, trying out different facial expressions and poses. His adrenaline was pumping in anticipation of how the girls would react, and he tried to imagine how the scene would play out. Would Callie kiss him right then and there? Would she say she wasn't interested? What would Olivia think when she saw him?

"I can't believe I'm rooming with a goddamn transvestite," Zeke said.

Max turned and faced him. "You know you love it. Come on, let's go."

"I should be high for this," Zeke said as they left their room and headed upstairs.

* * *

"Traitor," Olivia said as Mimi came rushing back to prepare her suitemates for the grand entrance. "I can't believe you've been helping the enemy."

"He's not the enemy," Mimi protested.

"I can't wait to see this," Trish said.

"You're not going to believe how good he looks." She turned to Callie. "Better get ready to pucker up."

"Yeah, right," Callie said. "Like I'm really going to kiss him."

"You might when you see him," Mimi said.

Olivia put her hands on Callie's shoulders and looked her in the eyes. "Whatever happens, I'll still love you."

"Get out of here," Callie said, turning away with a laugh.

There was a knock on the door.

"Oh my God," Mimi said. "Is everyone ready?"

Olivia and Trish hurried onto one couch, and Callie settled on the other.

"Okay," Mimi said, barely able to contain her excitement. "Here we go."

She opened the door and stepped quickly to the side.

Max stepped into the room.

"Oh . . . my . . . God," Trish said.

"Wow," Olivia said, taking him in. Max's features seemed softer, his brown eyes even bigger, his lips fuller and juicier. "You make a good-looking girl, Max."

Callie stared at him, speechless.

Trish turned to Mimi. "He looks almost exactly like Maggie Gyllenhaal."

Mimi beamed. "He does, right?"

"So," Max said, smiling broadly at Callie. "Am I hot enough to get a kiss?"

"Shit," Callie muttered.

"That sounds like a yes to me," Mimi said.

Callie looked at Olivia and shrugged hopelessly.

"Go ahead," Olivia said, smiling.

Callie hesitated.

"We can go in the bedroom if you want privacy," Mimi said.

"I want to see this," Trish protested.

Max walked over to the couch and sat next to Callie, who scooted away and avoided looking at him.

"Come on, Callie," Mimi implored. "Look at how hot he is."

She turned, looked him up and down, shook her head in resignation, then leaned in and gave him a quick kiss.

"Yay," Mimi sang out as she and Trish began to clap.

Max smiled at Callie. "You can feel my breasts if you want."

"Okay, I'm done," she said, getting up from the couch and walking into her bedroom.

"I'd like to feel them," Zeke said.

Max patted the seat next to him. "Bring it on, big boy."

Later that night as he sat up in his room sharing a celebratory joint with Zeke, his cell phone rang. "Unbelievable," he said, looking at the caller ID. "Does he have a fucking marijuana detector?" He flipped open his phone. "Hi, Dad."

Meanwhile, upstairs, Olivia huddled with her suitemates plotting the next part of the unfolding drama.

CASTRATION CELEBRATION

Act 3, scene 3

(*Early morning. Dick sits alone outside Jane's house. Jane comes out, carrying her book bag. She sees Dick and walks quickly toward school. Dick comes up beside her.*)

DICK: Can I talk to you? Please?

JANE: There's nothing to talk about.

DICK: Please, Jane. Just give me five minutes.

JANE: What's the point?

DICK (*taking her arm, looking her in the eyes, and speaking urgently*): Please.

JANE: What do you want?

DICK: I made a mistake, Jane. I'm sorry. I wish I hadn't done it.

JANE (*bitterly*): Well, that makes two of us.

DICK (*with feeling*): I don't want to lose you, Jane. You're the best thing that's ever happened to me, and I'm miserable thinking it could be over. Please, just give me another chance. I promise I'll make it up to you.

JANE: Are you finished?

DICK: Look, I know it probably doesn't matter at this point, but just so you know, I didn't actually cheat on you. Yes, I lied. Yes, I acted like a jerk. Yes, I even went off with another girl. But nothing happened. She was drunk. I sat with her in a bathroom stall while she threw up. That's it.

JANE: It doesn't matter, Dick. You can do whatever you want now.

DICK: All I want is to be with you. Can't you understand that?

JANE: All I understand is that we had something special and you fucked it up.

DICK: You see. Even you admit it was special.

JANE: Well, I was wrong.

DICK: Don't say that. We belong together.

JANE: I don't belong to anyone.

DICK: That's not what I mean. Look, I can't explain it, but there's something between us that just clicks. It's like we complete each other.

JANE: That sounds like a line from a bad movie.

DICK (*laughing*): You see. Even now you can make me laugh.

JANE: I wasn't trying to be funny.

DICK: Look at us, Jane. We're both miserable. Don't you want to go back to the way things were?

JANE: It's too late for that.

DICK: It's never too late. (*starts to sing*)

"We Belong Together"

Odysseus, Penelope
Orpheus, Eurydice
Superman, Lois Lane
Spider-Man, Mary Jane

JANE: What are you doing? Are you singing to me?

Cleopatra, Antony
Harry, Ron, Hermione

Ernie, Bert; Barbie, Ken
Liz Taylor and a lot of men

JANE: What are you talking about?

Some things go together
I don't know why, but everyone knows
That when they're together, it's better
That's how it goes; that's how it goes

(*Jane starts to walk away. Dick cuts her off and
continues to sing.*)

Adam, Eve; Tarzan, Jane
Rosebud and Charles Foster Kane
Kermit the Frog, Miss Piggy
Shel Silverstein, The Giving Tree
Batman, Robin; John and Paul
Michael Jordan, basketball
Lancelot and Guinevere
A frat boy and a keg of beer

(*Dick takes her hands.*)

Some things go together
I don't know why, but everyone knows
That when they're together, it's better
That's how it goes; that's how it goes

(She pulls away. He dances in front of her.)

> Bonnie, Clyde; Cheech and Chong
> A hippie and a graphix bong
> Timothy Leary, LSD
> Hugh Hefner and pornography
> Romeo and Juliet
> Miss Manners, proper etiquette
> Dr. Watson, Sherlock Holmes
> X and Y chromosomes
> Father, Son, and Holy Ghost
> New Year's Eve, a champagne toast
> Jerry, Kramer, George, Elaine
> Mork and Mindy; Dick and Jane

> Some things go together
> I don't know why, but everyone knows
> That when they're together, it's better
> That's how it goes; that's how it goes

(Dick is so caught up in the song that he does not even notice that Jane is walking away, and that Sluggo and Biff have appeared and are watching with undisguised amusement.)

> Yeah, we belong together
> I don't know why, but it's easy to see
> That when we're together, it's better
> Jane, I need you, and, Jane, you need me

SLUGGO (*applauding*): "Freebird."

DICK (*looking around*): Where's Jane?

BIFF: She left your ass. Can't really blame her.
(*singing to mock Dick*) We belong together. I need
you and you need me.

SLUGGO: Give it up, Dick. Girls are pretty fucking
unforgiving when they catch you screwing around
behind their backs.

BIFF: Yeah, man, fuck it. There's plenty of other
girls out there.

DICK: I don't want any other girls.

SLUGGO: WHAT?!

DICK: I'm through screwing around.

BIFF: Take that back, Dick.

DICK: I mean it. I'm done messing around. The only
girl I want is Jane.

(*Sluggo and Biff look at each other in stunned
silence.*)

SLUGGO: You're not serious.

DICK: I've never been more serious in my life.

(*Sluggo and Biff look at each other. They speak as though in a trance.*)

SLUGGO: Well.

BIFF: Yeah.

SLUGGO: I don't know what to say.

BIFF: Yeah.

DICK: How about good luck?

SLUGGO: Sure, Dick. Good luck.

BIFF: Yeah.

DICK: Thanks, guys. I'm gonna need it. (*He exits.*)

(*They stand for a while in deep thought.*)

SLUGGO: It's like the end of an era.

BIFF: I feel like a part of me has died.

SLUGGO: He was a great man.

BIFF: An inspiration to us all.

(*They stand for a long moment in silent tribute.*)

BIFF: Have you ever banged a Spanish chick?

SLUGGO: No.

BIFF: Me neither.

SLUGGO: We should do that sometime.

BIFF: Definitely. (*They exit.*)

(*Curtain*)

CHAPTER TWELVE

Max sat in a chair facing his examiners. Across the table, Mimi, Callie, and Trish stared back at him without speaking, each holding a pad of paper and a pen.

"This feels like a parole hearing," he said.

Callie smiled, not so much in a warm, encouraging way, but rather in a way that said, "You have no idea what you're in for, mister, and I'm going to enjoy watching you wriggle and squirm."

Olivia stood off to the side with a grim expression.

"Are you ready?" Mimi asked.

Max smiled. "Bring it on."

Mimi scanned her paper. "Okay," she said, "first question. Why should Olivia go out with you?"

Max took a moment to gather his thoughts and figure out how to begin. "I think we just have this amazing chemistry," he said to Mimi. "You've seen it, haven't you?" He looked at the other girls. "Olivia told me on the first night that she wasn't dating anyone this summer, and almost a month later, instead of moving on to someone else, I'm still trying to convince her. I got up in the middle of dinner and talked about being castrated for her. I spent hundreds of dollars being made over as a girl for her." He smiled at Callie. "Though being able to say that a lesbian kissed me is pretty cool."

Callie did not smile back.

"Anyway," he said. "I just think that we belong together."

Off to the side, Olivia suppressed a giggle and struggled to maintain a straight face.

"Next question," Trish said. "Are you looking for a committed relationship, or just some summer fun?"

"This isn't about just hooking up," Max said, "if that's what you're asking. I want Olivia to be my girlfriend."

"Until the program ends, or after that, too?"

"I don't know," Max said. "I guess we would have to see how we feel when the time comes."

"Well, what's the longest relationship you've ever been in?" Trish pursued.

The answer was two months, but the only reason it had even lasted that long was because Jenny had been sick with mono for three weeks in the middle. Were they trying to label him commitment-phobic?

"A little less than three months," he said, hoping this small embellishment would tip the scales in his favor.

"Were you completely monogamous the whole time?" Callie asked.

"I was," he said. Then he chuckled, thinking about how often he had pleasured himself while she was sick.

Callie pounced. "What's so funny?"

He shook his head. "Never mind."

"Well, why were you laughing?"

"It's nothing."

She glared at him. "How do we know you're not holding something back from us?"

"You don't," he said. "You'll just have to trust me." He held Callie's gaze until Mimi broke the impasse.

"Ask the next question, Callie," she said.

Callie looked down at her paper. "Do you think gay marriage should be legalized?"

"I do," Max said, without hesitation. "And I'm not just saying that because you're a lesbian."

"Do you have any gay friends?"

"Besides you?"

Callie did not respond or even smile.

"Not many," Max admitted. "But I wish I had more."

"Would you care if your kid was gay?"

"No, as long as he was happy. I would just worry about him being harassed is all." He smiled at Callie in a way meant to communicate that he was on her side.

"Do you ever tell gay jokes?"

He took a moment to think about the jokes he recycled most frequently. "Sometimes," he admitted, "but certainly no more than black, Jewish, or handicapped ones." He gave an embarrassed smile. "I guess I'm an equal opportunity offender."

"Equal opportunity offender," Callie said, writing on her pad.

"Okay," Mimi said. "Suppose you were going out with a girl,

and she told you that she was waiting until she got married to have sex. Would you stay with her?"

"Absolutely," Max said. "If I liked her enough." And assuming blow jobs were still on the table.

"What if all she would do was kiss?" Mimi asked.

Crap, he thought. "Is she a good kisser?"

"Let's say she is."

"I'd probably take a lot of cold showers."

Mimi and Trish laughed, and even Callie had trouble suppressing a grin.

"I have another question," Trish said. "What do you think is the most important element in a successful relationship?"

"You mean besides the sex?"

This time nobody laughed.

"I'm just kidding," he said quickly. "Let's see. The most important, most important—I guess I would have to say honesty."

"Honesty?" Callie said.

Max nodded.

"Great, then tell us. Do you ever surf the Web for porn?"

Did I say honesty? he thought. I meant communication. He put on his most sheepish expression. "I have, but hardly ever."

"Have you ever watched a pornographic movie or read a pornographic magazine?"

"In my life?" he said.

Callie nodded.

"Yes."

"In the past six months?"

Max searched his memory. "Not that I recall," he said.

"What about looked at porn online?"

He screwed up his face in mock concentration. "Probably."

"Would you say that you enjoy looking at pornography?"

Sweet Jesus, he thought, give me a break. He looked down at the table. "I do enjoy it, yes."

Callie smiled in victory. "No further questions."

"Are we done?" Max asked, surprised.

"Not quite," Mimi said. She looked at Trish.

"Last question," Trish said. She paused dramatically. "Remember about a week ago when I saw you coming back from being out all night?"

Max tensed, knowing what was coming and wishing it wasn't.

"What exactly did you do that night and who were you with?"

Fuck, he thought. Should he lie and risk getting caught? Should he tell the truth and hope they would understand? Either he delivered the performance of his life right now, or it could all be over. Looking directly at the girls across from him, he took a deep breath and began: "I said the most important thing in a successful relationship is honesty, so I'm going to be totally honest right now." He paused and turned toward Olivia. "I made a mistake," he said simply. "I wish I could take it back, but I can't."

She kept her face impassive, and he continued to address her.

"When I saw you at the movie that night with Bruce, after you had told me that you weren't dating boys this summer, something in me snapped. I left campus and just wandered around downtown feeling angrier and angrier, and then I remembered I had the phone number of a girl I had met on the train coming here. I don't know why I still had it; I wasn't planning on calling her. But I guess I was just feeling so hurt and angry and jealous." He frowned and turned back to Trish and Callie. "Anyway, she invited me to a party, and I had way too much to drink, and . . ." He shrugged. "The whole thing was stupid."

"Did you have sex with her?" Trish asked.

He took a deep breath and nodded slowly. "But only because I was so drunk and feeling so hurt. It didn't mean anything."

There was total silence in the room. Finally, Olivia stepped forward, faced Max without expression, and spoke in a strong voice that did not waver. "This concludes the interview. Mimi, Callie, and Trish are all going to vote now. If two of them vote yes, then I agree to end my boycott and go out with you. If two of them vote no, then you agree not to pursue me for the rest of the summer."

Max nodded solemnly. "I understand."

Olivia turned to Mimi. "Mimi, what is your vote?"

"I know how much you like Olivia," Mimi said, smiling at Max, "and I think it was, like, really brave of you to be so honest about what you did. I vote 'yes.'"

Max smiled, but did not speak a word.

"Callie?"

"As boys go, you're not terrible, but the fact is that you tell gay jokes even though you say you're not homophobic, you enjoy looking at porn, and you ran off and had sex with some random girl. You say that it didn't mean anything. That's not a justification. All it shows is that you see girls as sex objects, not as real people with feelings. I vote 'no.'"

Max felt his muscles tighten.

"So it comes down to this," Olivia said. "Trish?"

Trish looked down at her pad, and then met Max's eyes. "This is a big decision I have, Max, and I want you to know that I'm taking it very seriously."

He offered a tight smile and nodded.

"First of all, congratulations on even making it to the interview. I didn't think you'd be able to get this far. You showed a lot of resourcefulness to get here, and I have to say, you held up pretty well under pressure tonight." She looked back at her pad. "So let's examine the facts. You did have sex with another girl, but obviously it wasn't premeditated and obviously you regret having done it." She met Max's eyes. "Truthfully, since you and Olivia were never going out, there was technically nothing wrong with what you did. It certainly isn't like you cheated on her."

Right, Max thought. He felt himself starting to relax a little.

"On the other hand, as Callie said, it is pretty disrespectful to have sex with a girl and say it didn't mean anything. And the way you acted when you saw Olivia with another boy shows that you can definitely be paranoid, impulsive, and reckless."

She paused, and Max had to remind himself to breathe.

"I like you, Max. The question, though, is not whether I like you, but whether you and Olivia are right for each other." She looked at him for a long time. "Although it pains me to do this, I have to do what I think will be best for Olivia in the long run."

Max felt his heart fall into his stomach.

"My vote is 'no.'"

He looked at Olivia.

"I'm sorry, Max," Olivia said. "The verdict is final." Then she walked into her bedroom and closed the door.

CASTRATION CELEBRATION
Act 4, scene 1

(*One week later. Jane and Amber sit in Jane's room.*)

JANE: I'm telling you. He's driving me crazy.

AMBER: I think it's romantic. Flowers and love notes every day. I wish someone treated me like that.

JANE: Trust me, you don't. I'm practically ready to go out with him again just so he'll stop harassing me.

AMBER: Are you thinking about it?

JANE: I don't know. Maybe.

AMBER: You know what you should do? Give him a test and make him prove himself. You know the story of Jacob and Rachel from the Bible?

JANE: Since when do you read the Bible?

AMBER: I'm trying to become more spiritual.

(*Jane laughs.*)

AMBER: Do you want to hear the story or not?

JANE (*amused*): Sure.

AMBER: Jacob wanted to marry Rachel so much that he agreed to work for her father for seven years. Then, her father screws him over and gives him Rachel's sister instead. So Jacob's like, what the hell, and the father says, all right, you can have the one you want, but only if you work for me for another seven years. And you know what? He did it. Fourteen years just to get the girl he loved.

JANE: I'm not waiting fourteen years to have sex again.

AMBER: Why not? You waited seventeen years before you had it the first time.

JANE: Listen to you. I bet you couldn't even go seventeen hours without it.

AMBER: For your information, I haven't slept with anybody for over a month. It's all part of my new self-improvement plan.

JANE: No wonder you've been so grumpy lately.

AMBER: That's not very nice.

JANE: I'm just kidding. I'm proud of you. Really.

(*Sam knocks on the door.*)

JANE: Who is it?

SAM: It's me.

JANE: Come in.

(*Sam walks in, smiles at Amber, and looks away.*)

AMBER: Hi, handsome.

SAM (*blushing, holds out a wrapped present to Jane*): Dick asked me to give you this.

JANE (*taking the present and turning to Amber*): Can you believe this? He's got my little brother working for him now.

SAM: I think you should take him back.

JANE: Did he tell you to say that? Unbelievable.

AMBER: Open it.

(*Jane rips the paper and a small book falls out. Jane starts to laugh.*)

AMBER: What is it?

JANE: *Pat the Bunny.*

AMBER (*confused*): The baby book? Why did he send you that?

SAM: Maybe he wants to have a baby with you.

AMBER (*devilishly*): What do you know about having babies, Sam?

JANE: Oh, leave him alone. (*to Sam*) Did he say anything to you when he gave you this? Was there anything he wanted you to tell me?

SAM: Like what?

JANE: I don't know. He just gave it to you and didn't say anything?

SAM: He said, "Can you give this to your sister for me?" Then he told me if anyone ever messed with me to let him know and he'd take care of it.

AMBER: Oooh. Tough guy. So what's the deal with the book?

JANE (*putting it on her desk*): Nothing. It's stupid.

AMBER: Hey, Sam, if you were in love with me, would you do fourteen years of hard labor to marry me?

SAM (*extremely embarrassed*): I don't know.

AMBER (*pretending to be offended*): You don't know?

JANE: Leave him alone.

AMBER: Am I bothering you, Sam?

SAM (*still embarrassed*): No.

JANE: Okay, Sam, you can go now.

(*Sam gets up and hurries to the door.*)

AMBER: Fourteen years, Sam. Think about it.

SAM (*without looking at her*): Bye. (*He exits.*)

JANE: Better be careful. He might take you up on it.

AMBER: I should be so lucky.

JANE: So, seriously, what should I do? I mean, is it pathetic that I'm even considering going out with him again?

AMBER: Do you still love him?

JANE: No.

AMBER: You don't?

JANE: I don't know. Maybe I do. It's all so complicated.

AMBER: Well, maybe you should give Dick some kind of test. At least to prove that he'll be faithful.

JANE: Like what? Ask him to wear one of those ankle surveillance bracelets so I can track him wherever he goes?

AMBER: That would work.

JANE: Seriously.

AMBER: Why don't you pay a prostitute to make a pass at him and see what he does? It's almost impossible for a guy to say no to a hot girl who wants to have sex with him.

JANE: I'm not going to pay a prostitute to have sex with him.

AMBER: Well, let's hope he says no then.

JANE: It's a ridiculous idea.

AMBER: Why?

JANE: Where am I going to find a prostitute?

AMBER: Yellow Pages.

JANE: Come on. What do you think I should do?

AMBER: I could make a pass at him, if you want.

JANE: You slut.

AMBER: No, seriously, we could set the whole thing up.

JANE: He knows we're best friends.

AMBER: That's what makes it so good. Watch, you play Dick, and I'll be me.

JANE: What?

AMBER: You're at your locker and I come up to you. (*pretending to talk to Dick*) Hey.

JANE: This is stupid.

AMBER: Come on, just play along.

JANE (*rolling her eyes*): Fine. (*as Dick*) Hi.

AMBER: You know, I think Jane's crazy not to take you back.

JANE (*as Dick*): Well, I did cheat on her, lie to her face, and act like a total asshole.

AMBER (*giving Jane a dirty look*): I really don't understand her sometimes. You know she throws out everything you send her?

JANE: I do not.

(*Amber gives Jane an exasperated look.*)

JANE (*as Dick*): She does?

AMBER: I said if anyone sent me all those love notes and flowers, I'd probably marry him. And you know what she said?

JANE (*as Dick*): What?

AMBER: She said, be my guest. (*Amber shakes her head and laughs.*)

JANE (*as Dick*): She said that?

AMBER (*leaning over and giving Jane a kiss on the cheek*): I think she's crazy.

JANE (*wiping her cheek and becoming herself again*): Oh my God, you slut.

AMBER: Look, I'm not going to do anything with him. If he tries something, I'll tell him to screw off. And if he doesn't try anything, you can take him back.

JANE: I feel sick.

AMBER: Sluggo Merk is having a party Saturday night. We'll do it then.

JANE: I'm not going to a party at Sluggo's house.

AMBER: You don't have to. It wouldn't work if you were there.

JANE: What are you planning to do?

AMBER: I don't know. But believe me, I have plenty of experience coming on to guys.

JANE: That's what scares me.

AMBER: Oh, would you relax. You think I'm gonna make out with your boyfriend?

JANE: What if Dick's not there?

AMBER: Sluggo's one of his best friends. He'll be there. Now stop worrying so much. The worst thing that could happen is that Dick will try to kiss me, and then you'll know you were right not to get back together with him.

JANE: It doesn't feel right.

AMBER: Do you have a better idea?

JANE: I don't know.

AMBER: Look, you obviously miss him and the only reason you haven't taken him back is because you're

scared he'll hurt you again. This is a perfect way
to see if he's changed.

JANE (*hesitantly*): I guess.

AMBER: Trust me. What could possibly go wrong?

(*Curtain*)

CHAPTER THIRTEEN

When three days had passed and Max had offered little more than a curt greeting to her when their paths happened to cross, Olivia opened a blank document on her computer and wrote a new version of one of her songs.

"We Belong Together" (remixed)

Bathroom floor, Ajax
Filthy rich, unpaid tax
Porno, fake climax
Redneck, congealed earwax

Constipation, Ex-Lax,
Menstruation, Tampax
Terrorist, anthrax
Olivia and Mad Max

Some things go together
I don't know why, but everyone knows
Like England and bad weather
That's how it goes; that's how it goes

Adolf Hitler, Mussolini
Alcoholic, dry martini
Driving drunk, fierce collision
Little boys and circumcision

Richard Nixon, Watergate
Jim Crow South, segregate
Cheney, Rummy, Bush, Iraq
Slick Willy and his wily cock

Some things go together
I don't know why, but everyone knows
Like a horse's neck and tether
That's how it goes; that's how it goes

Catholic church, sex abuse
Ku Klux Klan and a noose
Texas, the electric chair
SUVs, polluted air

New Orleans, Hurricane Katrina
Brad and Jen and Angelina
Hair and lice, dog and flea
Me and Max, Max and me

Some things go together

I don't know why, but everyone knows

Like S and M and leather

That's how it goes; that's how it goes

Olivia thought back to the night she had hatched her plan for Max's interview. It had seemed so clever at the time, the kind of plot twist a good writer might come up with.

"You know the story of Jacob and Rachel from the Bible?" she had asked her suitemates, launching into a recounting of the tale. "The true test is what he does when everything falls apart for him."

"So we rig the outcome," Trish said.

Olivia sighed. " 'Rig' is such an ugly word."

"I don't know," Mimi said. "It doesn't seem fair."

"All's fair in love and war," Callie said.

"But the whole point of the interview is to see if he can be trusted. It doesn't make sense to hope that he'll go back on his word."

"Of course it doesn't," Olivia said. "But you have to be willing to break the rules when it really matters."

Trish nodded. "Like we're about to do."

Olivia smiled. "Exactly."

So in the end Max had failed. Instead of fighting for what he wanted, he had faded away with barely a whimper. So much for breaking rules and following your heart. Didn't he understand that the moment the bubble bursts is merely the climax, not the resolution? Shouldn't he have realized that when things hit rock bottom, that's when the protagonist must stand tall and prove himself? Couldn't he see the dramatic possibilities he had been presented with? How disappointing for it to end this way.

And with Max having exited stage left, Olivia found that she was struggling to figure out what to write. Should Dick and Jane end up together? She was getting to a point in her story where she needed to figure this out, and the situation with Max was making her feel less and less sure of what the answer should be. She stared at the notes on her computer screen.

REASONS THEY SHOULD END UP TOGETHER

The audience expects a happy ending.

It would show how each character has grown—Dick has learned what true commitment means, and Jane has learned to transcend her anger and to forgive.

It would parallel the story of Beatrice and Benedick.

As angry and hurt as Jane is, she still likes him.

REASONS THEY SHOULD NOT END UP TOGETHER

It would be a jolt to those expecting a happy ending.

The play is called *Castration Celebration,*
for crying out loud!

Because, in the end, boys will let you
down.

It would send a strong feminist
message that girls don't need boys to
be happy.

Art should imitate life.

She was still staring at her computer screen fifteen minutes later when her cell phone rang, and she saw that it was a call from home. Okay, she thought. She could use a diversion.

"Hi," she said, picking up.

"Is this an okay time?" her mother asked, a note of apology in her voice.

"Yeah, it's fine."

"Are you sure, because I could call back later if it's not?"

God, why was she so annoying? "It's fine, Mom, really."

Olivia waited for her mom to say something, and began to tense up as the silence stretched to several seconds.

"So how are you, sweetie?" her mother asked at last. "How's the writing going?"

"Everything's going fine, Mom," Olivia said, standing up and beginning to pace.

More silence. Something was definitely wrong.

"Are you okay, Mom?"

She heard her mother sniffle.

"Mom, what's wrong? Is it Lucy?" The thought that her sister had gotten into real trouble flashed through her mind.

"No, Lucy's fine," her mother said in a quavering voice.

She felt a momentary surge of relief, which quickly turned to anger. "Did something happen with Dad?"

Her mother started to cry.

"Mom, what happened?"

"I'm sorry," her mother said. "I shouldn't have called you."

"It's okay, Mom," she said, impatience and concern mingling in her voice. "Just tell me what happened."

There was a long silence, and then her mother said, "Your father and I had a fight. That's all. It's over now."

"What did he do?"

"Nothing. Nothing new. I just thought, maybe . . ." She stopped.

"Is he home now?"

She did not answer.

"I don't know why you put up with it," Olivia said. "Why don't you just divorce him?"

"It's not that easy. You're too young to understand, but—"

"Too young to understand what?" Olivia said angrily. "That Dad cheats on you with girls half his age, and you don't do anything about it?"

Her mother began to cry again, and Olivia pulled the phone away from her ear, clenched it in her hand, and screwed up her face. She took several deep breaths and then put the phone back to her ear.

"I'm sorry, Mom," she said in a softer tone. "I shouldn't have said that."

"It's okay," her mother said, tapering down to a few sniffles. "I shouldn't have called you. I just wanted to hear your voice is all."

Olivia pictured her mother sitting alone at the kitchen table with her cup of tea, and she felt a lump rising in her throat. Was it okay that she had left for the summer, with her father off screwing younger girls, Lucy becoming more rebellious, and her mother sinking deeper and deeper into her shell? Her fucking father. It was his fault that the family was falling apart.

"Are you sure you're okay, Mom? I could come home if you want." Please no, she thought.

"Oh, honey, I would never ask you to do that. You enjoy the rest of your program."

"It's only two more weeks," Olivia said.

"Twelve days," her mother said, with a little laugh. "Not that I'm counting."

When Olivia got off the phone, she grabbed her keys and wallet, and walked quickly down the hall, down the stairs, and out into the evening air. She couldn't be cooped up anymore or her head might explode. Moving briskly out the campus gate onto Elm Street, she turned right and walked away from Broadway, where everybody from the program would be. She didn't know where she was going, it was just one step after another, pushing forward mindlessly. Her sandals slapped the sidewalk, and the steady smack of her steps filled her head. This was what she wanted, to clear her head, to pound out the anger and guilt and resentment and sadness without having to think about or visualize what was behind it.

She didn't know how long she had been walking, but the day's light was starting to fade as she found herself crossing the New Haven Green. Her mind had settled into a state of quiet reflection. Musing on the phone call, she realized that nothing had changed at home, and her being there for the summer wouldn't have made a difference. Her parents were grown-ups, and they could deal with their own problems. And she had been right not to get involved with Max this summer. Who knew if he would have stayed faithful? What was clear was that any emotional attachment would have made her life more complicated. She had twelve days left to finish her musical, and she intended to eke out every moment she had left to produce the best piece of work she could possibly produce.

A familiar-looking figure was walking ahead of her, and she realized with a jolt that it was Zeke. She called his name, but he did not stop or turn around. His head was bent as he walked, like he was counting his steps or trying not to step on cracks.

"Hey," she said, rushing to catch up and tapping him on the shoulder.

He looked like someone coming out of a trance. "Oh, hi," he said, without a trace of emotion.

"Didn't you hear me calling you?" she said.

He shook his head. "No."

"We need to get together soon to work on the play. Maybe tomorrow afternoon."

Zeke did not respond.

"Are you okay?" she asked, looking hard at him.

"Yeah."

"You seem kind of distracted."

"I'm just tired," he said.

"Are you sure?"

He nodded. "I've got to go."

She watched him walk off and wondered what was going on with him. This was turning into a strange night. First her mother, now Zeke . . . what next? Mimi suddenly deciding to go goth? Max turning out to be gay?

Still feeling a little off-kilter, she went to class the next morning, steeling herself to spend three hours in the same room as Bruce. It was true he had stopped stalking her ever since she had fake come out to him as a lesbian, but his behavior in class had become increasingly obnoxious, and this morning he was in rare form.

Maxine was leading a discussion about theme.

"What is your play really about?" she asked the class. "It's not enough to say 'family' or 'friendship' or 'love.' What ideas about these themes are you trying to get across?"

Of course Bruce was the first to answer. "My play is about how political correctness is a major threat to a free-thinking, democratic society."

Olivia rolled her eyes. Even if she agreed with him on some level, the way he looked so smug and self-righteous made her want to smack him.

"Interesting," Maxine said. "Would you care to elaborate?"

"People should be able to say whatever they think, even if other people might be offended. For example," he said, looking at Olivia and Trish, "I think girls should stop complaining about sexism. You all have it so much easier than guys."

"Are you crazy?" Trish cut in.

"See. I make one statement, and already you're jumping down my throat."

"It has nothing to do with being politically correct," Olivia said. "It has to do with your sounding like an idiot."

"Look at the facts," Bruce said calmly. "We have to work our asses off to get laid. You all just have to put on some tight clothes and shake your boobs around."

"You don't know what you're talking about," Trish said angrily.

"And then when we get older," he continued, "we're expected to support the family, while you all can sit around the house watching soap operas and getting fat. It's no wonder so many guys end up cheating."

He had no idea the hit he had scored, and Olivia wouldn't give him the satisfaction of seeing her lose control, but she resolved to make his dramatic counterparts suffer terribly when she started writing again.

At about six-thirty that evening as she was rereading her scene, Olivia heard a loud knock on her door and found Max standing outside.

"Have you seen Zeke?" he asked urgently.

"No, and I've actually been looking for him today."

"You have no idea where he is?"

Olivia's face registered concern. "Why? Did something happen?"

"I have no idea," Max said. "When I came back to the suite this afternoon, all his stuff was gone."

"What do you mean gone?"

"Gone. Like he packed up and left."

"Oh my God," Olivia said. "Did you call his cell phone?"

Max nodded. "It just goes straight to voice mail."

"Does Shakespeare know?"

"He's not around. And I don't want to start some crazy manhunt until I know he's missing."

"When did all this happen?" Olivia asked.

"He was still in the room when I left for class this morning. I didn't come back until about an hour ago, because I was rehearsing a scene this afternoon."

"Okay, this is a little bit freaky," she said. "I saw him last night on the Green, and he seemed really out of it."

"What was he doing?"

"Nothing, just walking, you know, but when I called him he didn't hear me, and then he seemed really distracted when I was talking to him."

"Did he say anything?"

"Just that he was tired." She looked at Max. "Do you think he really took off without telling anyone?"

"That's what it looks like."

"He didn't leave a note or anything?"

Max shook his head. "Nothing."

"Does anyone have his home number?" Olivia asked.

It was just a moment, and they both called out, "Trish!"

"Where is she?" Max asked.

"At dinner, I think."

"Okay," Max said. "I'm going to go look."

"I'll come," she said. "Let me put on some shoes."

She ran into her bedroom, grabbed her sandals, and hurried out, forgetting in her haste even to put her computer to sleep.

```
CASTRATION CELEBRATION
Act 4, scene 2


(Biff sits alone onstage. Music starts and he
begins to sing.)


          "I Saw My Parents Having Sex"


       I've seen blood and I've seen gore
       And I would see a whole lot more
          If only I could run away
         From what I saw the other day
          I saw my parents having sex


        I know I wasn't supposed to be
         Home until a half-past three
         A twist of fate, a fatal quirk
        Why weren't Mom and Dad at work?
          I saw my parents having sex


         You may say it's scientific
         Let me tell you, it's horrific
         I know it's how I came to be
       But it's not something I should see
```

There is nothing quite so gruesome
As my parents in a twosome
There is nothing quite so vile
As Dad on Mom, doggy-style

To be an orphan would be sad
And divorce hurts really bad
But when your parents are divorced
You don't walk in on intercourse
I saw my parents having sex

Can you believe I saw them naked?
Saw the grass where my dad's snake hid
Maybe if my mom was hot
I'd suck it up, but she is not
I saw my parents having sex

You may say it's scientific
Let me tell you, it's horrific
I know it's how I came to be
But it's not something I should see
There is nothing quite so gruesome
As my parents in a twosome
There is nothing quite so vile
As Dad on Mom, doggy-style

(*Sluggo rushes excitedly onstage and music stops abruptly.*)

SLUGGO: Biff, you're not gonna believe this.

BIFF: No, dude, you're not gonna believe this.

SLUGGO: What?

BIFF: No, you first.

SLUGGO (*excitedly*): My parents are staying in New York till Sunday night.

BIFF (*without much enthusiasm*): Oh, cool.

SLUGGO: Cool? It rocks. This party's gonna be legendary.

(*Biff just nods.*)

SLUGGO: Dude, what's with you?

BIFF (*looking at Sluggo intently*): I saw my parents having sex.

SLUGGO (*unable to stifle a laugh*): Are you serious? When?

BIFF (*shaking his head, obviously pained by the recollection*): Remember how I cut out of school early yesterday?

SLUGGO: Oh, Jesus.

BIFF: So I get home, right? And I'm going up to my room, and my parents' door is open, and I hear noises.

SLUGGO (*incredulous*): You went in?

BIFF: It was the middle of the day. They were supposed to be at work.

SLUGGO: This is unbelievable.

BIFF: Dude, it was awful.

SLUGGO: What? What did you see?

BIFF: Doggy-style.

SLUGGO: NO!

BIFF: Yes.

SLUGGO: What did you do?

BIFF: I couldn't move. Like when you see a car crash, you know, and you can't turn away even though there's blood and bodies everywhere. I just stood there, and then my mom started to scream, and my dad

yelled at me to get the fuck out. I took off and
didn't come home last night until after they were
asleep.

SLUGGO: Jesus.

BIFF: Then this morning, I try to get out of the
house without seeing them, but they're waiting for
me like goddamn vultures, and my dad tells me to sit
down, we have to have a talk, and I'm like, "Dad,
I've got to go," and he grabs me and says (*in
father's voice*), "Sit your ass down in that chair."
My mom starts to cry, and my dad's like, "You see
how you've upset your mother." Then he starts giving
me a goddamn lecture about not barging into other
people's rooms without knocking and how would I like
it if he barged into my room without knocking. So I
say, "But you didn't even have your door closed,"
and that just sets him off again. "Well, why weren't
you in school? No wonder you're getting Ds in all
your classes. Do you like to cut school so you can
sneak home and look through your mother's underwear
drawers? What are you, some kind of fucking
pervert?"

SLUGGO (*incredulous*): He said that?

BIFF: My mom's totally hysterical at this point, and
she starts to scream at my dad to stop, but he's on

216

a roll. (*in father's voice*) "What else do you do? Do you jack off in our bed? Is that what you do? You come home early, find a pair of your mother's panties, and jack off in our bed?"

SLUGGO: Jesus.

BIFF: It gets worse. My mom runs out of the room, and my dad goes totally ape-shit. (*in father's voice*) "Do you like to fuck sheep, too? Is that what you like, you goddamn pervert, always talking about fucking sheep? Oh, yeah, you think I don't hear the shit you and your friends talk about?"

SLUGGO (*laughing*): He's got you there.

BIFF: So finally he tires himself out and goes off to look for my mother, and I bolt. (*pause*) What am I gonna do?

SLUGGO: There's really only one thing you can do. Get totally hammered and party your ass off.

BIFF: I better get laid tonight is all I can say.

SLUGGO: Sorry, man. No sheep allowed.

BIFF (*laughing*): Fuck you.

(*Dick walks onstage.*)

SLUGGO: There he is. Mr. Monogamy.

DICK: Mr. Celibacy is more like it. What's going on, guys?

SLUGGO: Getting ready to do a little partying.

DICK: I hear you.

SLUGGO: You hear that Biff walked in on his parents boning?

DICK (*turning to Biff*): No!

BIFF: I don't want to talk about it.

DICK: You actually walked in while your parents were having sex?

BIFF: I really don't want to talk about it.

DICK: You need to get yourself good and drunk, my friend. Wipe that picture right out of your mind.

SLUGGO: You want to come by early tonight, Dick? Get a little head start on the festivities?

DICK: Sorry, man, can't do it. Got some shit I need to take care of.

SLUGGO: You are coming to the party, though.

DICK (*hesitating*): We'll see. I've got this family thing—

SLUGGO: Bullshit. You think I'm some dumb chick you're talking to? You don't come to my party tonight and I'm gonna go medieval on your ass.

DICK (*laughing*): All right, man. I'll be there.

SLUGGO: And no moping around talking about Jane all night, either. It's fucking depressing, you know.

DICK: Any other rules I should know about?

BIFF: Yeah. Everybody gets drunk, and everybody gets laid.

SLUGGO: But no fucking sheep.

DICK (*smiling*): All right, fellas, I'll catch you later.

BIFF: Later.

(*Dick exits.*)

SLUGGO: Can you believe that? He was gonna blow off the party. I mean, what the fuck?

BIFF: Can we just go start drinking? Because right now I've got this picture in my head of my dad humping my mom, and it's starting to freak me out.

SLUGGO (*ignoring Biff*): Thinks he can pull that family shit on me. Who the hell does he think he's dealing with?

BIFF (*now also lost in his own thoughts*): Riding her like a horse.

SLUGGO: I was using that story before he ever was.

BIFF: Tits flouncing all over the place.

SLUGGO: Fuck him.

BIFF: (*in high-pitched voice*): "Fuck me, fuck me."

SLUGGO (*looking at Biff*): What the fuck are you talking about?

BIFF (*embarrassed*): Nothing.

SLUGGO: Holy shit, is that a boner?

BIFF (*extremely embarrassed, turning away*): No.

SLUGGO (*laughing, incredulous*): Did you just get hard thinking about your parents?

BIFF: No.

SLUGGO (*shaking his head*): You're sick, man.

BIFF (*angrily*): Would you shut up?

SLUGGO: You really do sniff your mom's panties, don't you?

BIFF (*charging at Sluggo and tackling him*): I told you to shut up!

(*Biff and Sluggo grapple with each other on the floor, with neither one getting the upper hand. The wrestling begins to take on a more sexual nature, until it's hard to tell whether the boys are fighting or humping each other. Sluggo pins Biff and lies on top of him. They stare into each other's eyes, and suddenly Sluggo leans down and kisses Biff on the mouth. Biff pushes Sluggo off and leaps up. They stare at each other in horror.*)

SLUGGO (*pleadingly*): Biff—

(*Biff shakes his head, horrified, then turns and runs away.*)

(*Curtain*)

CHAPTER FOURTEEN

"Shit," Trish said.

Max looked at her. "What?"

"I'm getting pulled over."

Max spun around and spotted the police car behind them with its light flashing. "You sure are," he said.

"How fast were you going?" Olivia asked.

"About eighty, I think." She slowed to a stop on the shoulder of the highway, and the police car pulled up behind her. Through her rearview mirror, she watched the officer approach her car. He was a stocky guy, sporting sunglasses, a mustache, and a stomach that had seen a few too many jelly donuts. She brushed her hair back and took a deep breath.

"License and registration," he said.

Trish handed them over, and he walked back to his car to run them through his database.

"You don't have any drugs in here, do you?" Max asked.

"No. Of course not."

"Too bad," he said with a smile.

"You better not do something stupid and get us arrested," Trish said.

Max patted her shoulder reassuringly. "Relax."

The police officer returned to the car and handed Trish her papers. "Are you aware that you were driving eighty-three in a sixty-five zone?"

"I'm sorry," Trish said. "I didn't realize I was going so fast."

He leaned over and looked in the car window. "Are you kids in a hurry to get somewhere?"

"We're on a mission from God," Max said, and Trish could not suppress a laugh.

Perhaps the officer had never seen *The Blues Brothers.* Perhaps he had seen it and was not amused by the film's portrayal of the police force. Whatever the case, he did not even crack a smile. "Would you all step out of the car, please?" There was not a trace of humor in his voice.

"We're on our way to a funeral," Trish said.

"Step out of the car."

They stood there on the side of the highway while the officer questioned them. Max was tempted to wave to the people in the cars speeding by, but restrained himself. No sense giving Officer McJelly any more reason to detain them. He seemed disappointed enough already that he had not been able to uncover any illegal substances.

"You kids keep driving like that and people will be coming to *your* funerals," he said before walking back to his car.

"What an asshole," Max said as they set off again. "I'll split the ticket with you."

"We can all split it," Olivia said.

"We're on a mission from God." Trish chuckled. "That was priceless."

"You remember they end up in *jail* in the movie," Olivia said.

Max laughed. "He wasn't going to arrest us."

"I think I'm going to put a jail scene in my play," Trish said.

Olivia looked thoughtful. "You know," she said, "that's actually not a bad idea."

The church was packed tight by the time they got there, and they found seats near the back. Afterward, they waited outside until Zeke emerged. He was with a few other boys, all of them in suits, looking somber and grim.

"I feel weird being here," Olivia said. "We didn't even know him."

"We're here for Zeke," Max said. "Look, he sees us."

Zeke said something to the boys he was with and walked slowly over.

Trish stepped forward and gave him a hug, which he barely reciprocated. "We weren't sure we should come, but it felt weird to stay."

"I'm so sorry," Olivia said, reaching out and squeezing his hand.

Max looked at his roommate. "How are you holding up?"

Zeke shrugged. "I'm okay."

"You should have told me," Trish said. "I would have driven you here."

"The whole thing is so sad," Olivia said. "I didn't even know him, and I still cried."

All around them, people were getting into cars and driving off. The boys Zeke had been with walked past, and one of them said they would wait in the car.

"I've got to go," Zeke said.

"We can give you a ride to the cemetery," Trish said.

Zeke shook his head. "It's okay."

"Well, we'll follow you then," Max said.

"Why?" Zeke asked, his voice tinged with irritation. "You didn't even know him."

"I did," said Trish.

"Not really." Zeke started to walk away.

"Wait," Max said.

Zeke turned. "What?" he said impatiently.

"Where can we meet you after, then?"

Zeke shook his head. "I don't even know why you came."

"You left without telling anyone," Max said. "You took all your stuff."

"We were worried," Olivia added. "I mean, you disappeared right in the middle of us working on the musical."

"Fuck the stupid musical!" Zeke practically shouted. "My best friend just died."

"Take it easy," Max said.

"I'm out of here." Zeke stormed off toward the parking lot, and they stood there watching him in stunned silence.

"Well, that sucked," Max finally said.

Olivia looked like she was ready to cry.

"He didn't mean it," Max said, putting his hand on her shoulder.

Olivia shrugged him off. "Let's just go back to New Haven. There's no point staying. I don't even know why we came."

Why had they come? Max wondered. If Zeke had wanted or needed them, he would have told them he was leaving. But then, when Trish had reached a friend back home and found out what had happened, it had just seemed so important to come and offer Zeke support. Max had been filled with the righteousness of the venture, as if, somehow, they were rescuing Zeke from something dark and terrible, though, in truth, Max had no idea what.

"What do you think?" Trish asked, hurt and disappointment mingling on her face and in her voice.

"I don't know," he said helplessly.

They walked slowly toward Trish's car. She clicked the locks and they climbed in, with Max riding shotgun and Olivia in the back. "We could go back to my house for a while and try to call him after all of this is over."

"What's the point?" Olivia said. "He's not going to want to talk to us."

Trish started the engine, backed slowly out of her space, and joined the line of cars exiting the parking lot. "So, New Haven then?" she asked.

Nobody said anything. To Max, the thought of everything ending like this was beyond depressing. Was this really it? He was never going to see Zeke again? How much worse could the summer get? Rejected by Olivia, told to fuck off by Zeke, and now a four-hour car ride back to New Haven?

"I think we should at least stick around until all the funeral stuff is over," Max said.

Olivia groaned. "Let's just get back."

"Come on," Max said. "We have to talk to him."

"So call him tomorrow. He doesn't want to see us." Olivia sounded exasperated, like a parent explaining something to a particularly stubborn toddler for the umpteenth time.

"She's right, Max," Trish said in a defeated tone. "We might as well head back."

"We're just going to leave?"

"We tried," Olivia said, her frustration mounting. "We drove all the way here, didn't we? We almost got arrested, which, by the way, would have been your fault. We tried to talk to Zeke and got berated in front of a crowd of people. I'd say that's enough for one day, wouldn't you?"

Max turned in his seat. "You're just upset because he yelled at you."

"Yes, and because we wasted an entire day that I should have been working on my musical."

Max looked at Trish. "If you two want to go back to New Haven, you should go. I'll take a bus tonight or tomorrow."

"Come on," Trish said. "That's crazy."

"I'm not giving up so easily."

"Why not?" Olivia said. "You gave up pretty easily with me."

Max spun back toward her. "What the hell are you talking about?"

She looked him directly in the eye. "You don't even get it, do you?"

"What's there to get? I did every damn thing you asked me to. It's not my fault you need a committee to tell you who to date."

"Whoa, whoa, whoa," Trish cut in. "Both of you need to take a breath and chill out."

"Just drop me off at Zeke's house, and you can go," Max said, staring straight ahead.

"Come on, Max. I'm not really going to leave you here."

"Why not?" Olivia said. "It's what he wants."

"I'm not leaving him. Obviously the two of you have some issues to work out, and you need to deal with them before I spend the next four hours stuck in a car with you." She honked her horn at a green Volvo on a cross street that was already stopped at a stop sign waiting for her to turn. "We're going to my house, and you two can have an empty room to duke it out all you want, because I don't want to listen to this shit anymore."

"Sorry," Max said. He stared out his window, wondering how it was possible he had liked Olivia so much in the first place.

CHAPTER FIFTEEN

"Look," Max said as soon as they had closed the door to the downstairs bedroom. "I don't want to fight about this. You go back with Trish, and I'll fend for myself."

"Can't we just talk for a few minutes? I know you're angry at me, but I don't want to spend the rest of the summer not talking to each other."

"I thought that was exactly what you wanted. So you wouldn't be distracted from your precious play."

"I don't know what I want anymore." She came across the room and sat on the bed. "The last couple days have been really hard, and then when Zeke yelled at me—it was just too much."

"Well, you shouldn't have said anything about the musical."

"I know," Olivia said, tears starting again in her eyes. "I can't believe I was so stupid." She put her head in her hands and stared down at the floor.

Max came and sat on the bed, but did not touch her. After a few moments, he said quietly, "What did you mean in the car when you said I gave up on you?"

She shook her head.

"Tell me. I want to understand."

She looked up and sighed. "After the interview. You didn't keep trying. You just gave up on me."

"What do you mean?" he said. "It was over. You were the one who made the rules."

"I know." She nodded. "But maybe I wanted you to show that you would keep fighting for me. That you wouldn't just give up and run away when it got hard."

He looked at her, trying to absorb what she had just said. "So you wanted me to keep going even after they voted against me? To keep trying to get you to go out with me?"

"I don't know," she said. "Maybe."

He shook his head and stared at her. Was she totally mental?

"You probably think I'm totally mental," she said.

A smile crept across his face, and he started to nod.

"Maybe I am," she said with a little laugh. "You know, I actually set up the whole interview so there was no way you could win."

His smile disappeared. "What do you mean?"

"It was stupid," she said, already regretting bringing it up. "I just figured that if you didn't give up even after you failed the test, then you really must be committed."

He stood up and began to pace around the room. "Let me get this straight," he said. "No matter what I said in the interview, there was no way I could win? The whole thing was already rigged?"

"Don't get mad," she said.

"And Trish was part of this, too?"

"It was my idea. She just agreed to play along."

"You really *are* mental, you know that?" he said, turning and taking a step toward the door.

"Wait," she said. "Please."

He wanted to keep going, to say something harsh to Trish, and then to storm out of the house. But then what? What would he do? Where would he go? He had no idea where Zeke lived or how to get there.

He took a deep breath and turned back to Olivia. "I can't—"

"Just let me explain," she said.

"Explain what? Why you fucked with my head? Why you spend all your time cooped up in your room writing a play about castration? Let me guess. Your last boyfriend screwed your best friend, and this is your way of getting revenge."

She started to cry, almost silently, her mouth curling down, her eyes dripping tears.

Max watched her for a moment without compassion. She had hurt him, and he had hurt her back. But now that she was crying, he felt his anger begin to drain away. Maybe she had been right to worry about his commitment. It wasn't like he had such a great track record.

He crossed the room and sat next to her on the bed. "Okay," he said more gently, wrapping her in a hug. "Here. Let's stop fighting."

She allowed him to hold her for several seconds, and then she pushed him away. "That was a mean thing to say," she said.

He wiped a tear from her cheek and smiled at her. "I'm sorry."

"I'm sorry, too," she said after a moment. "It wasn't right what I did."

They sat there looking at each other, and Max started to laugh.

"What?" Olivia said.

Max shook his head. "Nothing."

"Tell me."

"I can't."

"Come on," she said, starting to smile.

He chuckled and shook his head. Could he say it? Oh, what the hell? "I was just thinking it would be funny if we had sex right now."

She stared at him, wide-eyed in disbelief.

"Seriously," he said quickly. "I've heard that makeup sex after a fight is amazing."

"Makeup sex? We've never had regular sex. We've never even kissed."

"So?"

Olivia stood up and walked away from the bed. "You're out of your mind."

"It might inspire you to write."

"What, we're going to have sex here in Trish's house while she's waiting for us in the other room and her parents might come home at any minute? That's a great idea."

"It *is* a great idea," Max said, gaining momentum. "The only thing better than makeup sex is makeup sex with the possibility of being walked in on."

She looked at him as though he were some alien life-form. "Are you for real?"

"Come on." Max patted the bed. "Let's do it."

"I'm leaving," Olivia said, walking to the door.

"It would make a great story."

"Goodbye," she said, walking out of the room.

Max jumped up and followed her out. Trish was sitting at the kitchen table drinking a Diet Coke.

"That was fast," she said. "Are we all friends again?"

"I don't know," Max said, draping an arm over Olivia's shoulder. "Are we?"

"Shut up." She shrugged him off and sat down next to Trish.

"This is a nice house," Max said, looking around.

"You want a tour?"

"Sure." He looked at Olivia. "Or are you in a rush to leave?"

"It's okay," she said.

They followed Trish out of the kitchen. On the way through the house they learned that Trish's dad liked dead British writers and pipes, and her mother had an absurdly large collection of dolls. They ended up in the attic, a large carpeted room with a home office, a treadmill, and assorted remnants of Trish's childhood, including three regional spelling bee trophies.

"This is where Zeke and I wrote most of our musical," Trish said.

Olivia looked at the stack of board games in the corner. "Maybe we *should* stay and try to talk to him."

Max looked at her. "Zeke? Really?"

"I don't know," Olivia said. "I guess if I'm going to get mad at you for giving up on me, it would be pretty stupid for me to give up on Zeke."

"I haven't given up on you," Max said.

Olivia rolled her eyes and turned to Trish. "Is it okay if we stay and try to see him later? You're the one driving."

Trish looked from one to the other and smiled. "It's okay with me. We can always stay here tonight and head back in the morning."

"Cool," Max said.

"Are you sure that will be okay with your parents?" Olivia asked.

"They're in California until next week."

"Interesting," Max said, looking meaningfully at Olivia.

Olivia ignored him, and they started back downstairs.

"Do you think there's any chance Zeke might come back for the end of the program?" Max asked as they settled in the living room.

Olivia shook her head. "He took all his stuff, remember?"

"I know," Max said, "but maybe we can convince him."

"I wish," Olivia said.

"Well, just don't start talking about the musical again when we see him," Trish said.

Olivia gave her an irritated look. "I'm not an idiot."

"I have an idea," Max said. "You know in *The Blues Brothers* when—"

"Oh, Jesus," Olivia said. "Here we go again."

"No, this is good, listen. You know the scene where they're

trying to get Mr. Fabulous to rejoin the band, and they go to that fancy restaurant where he's the maître d' and act all crazy to embarrass him?" He jumped into character. "I want to buy your women . . . the little girl . . . your daughters. Sell them to me. Sell me your children."

Olivia and Trish laughed, impressed by Max's spot-on imitation of John Belushi.

"So what if we do the same thing? Just hang around Zeke's house making a nuisance of ourselves until he agrees to come back to New Haven with us?"

"That's so mean," Olivia said. "His friend just died. Could you imagine if someone did that to you?"

This silenced them for several seconds.

"I'm going to call over there and see if Zeke's mom is home," Trish said, pulling out her cell. "I didn't see her at the funeral."

Max leaned over toward Olivia. "Thanks for doing this," he said.

Olivia nodded. "What are you going to say to him?"

"I don't know. Just improvise, I guess."

"Oh, right," she said. "You're an actor. You can do that."

"Most of the time," he agreed. "Though you didn't seem too impressed when I tried in the bedroom before."

She smiled. "You just need to work on your timing."

Twenty minutes later they were sitting in Zeke's living room, which had floor-to-ceiling bookshelves and a framed Andy Warhol print over the couch.

Max heard the front door open, and Zeke walked in.

"Surprise," Max said.

Zeke took in the scene and frowned. "What are you doing here?"

"Your friends came over to see you," his mother said. "Come sit with us."

He glared at her, then pulled a chair from the kitchen and sat down.

"How was the cemetery?" Max asked.

"Fine."

"Who was there?" his mother asked.

"A lot of people you don't know." He reached out, took a walnut from the bowl on the coffee table, and cracked it loudly with a nutcracker.

"I'm sorry about bringing up the musical at the funeral," Olivia said.

Zeke shrugged. "I shouldn't have gotten so angry."

"Olivia was telling me about it," his mother said. "It sounds hilarious."

"It is," Trish said.

"I loved the one you and Zeke did for school." She smiled at her son. "Remember that, honey?"

"No, Mom, I forgot."

There was a moment of uncomfortable silence, and then his mom said, "Must be all that pot you smoke." She winked at Max and got up. "I'll leave you all to talk. Help yourself to anything in the fridge."

She walked out of the room, and Max turned to Zeke. "Okay, I get it. If my dad was that cool, I'd want to stay home, too."

Olivia looked stupefied. "Did she really just say that?"

"Is she seeing anyone?" Max asked.

"What's the matter with you?" Zeke said.

"I'm just kidding around. Seriously, though, your mom is awesome."

"She is," Trish said.

"You don't have to live with her." Zeke took off his jacket and undid his tie, leaving it draped around his neck. "So you guys decided to come all the way up here and track me down?"

"Pretty much," Max said.

Zeke nodded. "I guess I should have said goodbye before I left."

"We were worried," Max said. "Every time I called your cell, it went straight to voice mail."

"I had my phone off," Zeke said. He reached into his jacket pocket, pulled out his cell, turned it on, and put it in the pocket of his pants. "I just wanted to get home without having to talk about it."

Olivia nodded sympathetically. "It must have been so hard to get that news. I can't even imagine."

He looked away, then stared at a spot on the coffee table. "I'm sorry about your musical," he said. "It was fun working on it."

"It's okay," Olivia said.

"I'm sure you can get someone else in my class to finish the music."

Olivia nodded. "I'll figure something out."

Zeke studied the walnuts in the bowl before selecting another one and cracking it open. "If you want, you can e-mail me the lyrics, and I'll work on them from here."

Olivia looked at him. "Really?"

Zeke nodded. "I need something to do, or I'll be climbing the walls."

"Why don't you come back to New Haven, then?" Max said.

Zeke made a sound that was somewhere between a laugh and a grunt.

"Seriously," Max said. "Who am I supposed to get high with if you don't come back?"

"I've had enough." His voice was tired, but firm and unwavering.

Everyone sat there looking at each other.

"There's nothing we can say to convince you?" Max asked.

Zeke shook his head.

"Well," Max said after a pause, "if this is really the last time we're going to see you, let's at least hang out tonight." He looked at Trish. "Are you still okay with leaving in the morning?"

"Okay with me," Trish said.

"I'm going to crash early tonight," Zeke said. "It's been a long couple of days."

"Yeah, maybe we should head back," Olivia said. "I need to get an early start working tomorrow."

"Come on," Max said. "What if we all go back to Trish's house and work on your play tonight? Trish's parents are away," he said to Zeke. "We can have an all-night jam session and knock this thing out."

"I'm not staying up all night," Trish said. "Not if we're driving back in the morning."

"So you'll turn in early, or we'll all share the drive back. Come on, it will be awesome. Haven't you ever pulled an all-nighter for school?"

"No," Olivia said.

"We almost did to finish our Bible musical," Trish said. "I could barely keep my eyes open the next day."

"We'll load up on caffeine." He turned to Zeke. "Hey, do you think you can get your hands on some speed?"

"No way," Trish said. "You're not turning my parents' house into a drug den."

"Speed?" Olivia looked at Max and shook her head. "Who are you?"

Max laughed. "Well, I've never actually done it, but I've heard that when people have to go without sleep for a couple of days it keeps them wired and going."

"Tell me again why we're not sleeping," Olivia said.

"We're going to finish your play tonight. Think about how psyched you'll be." He fixed Zeke with a gaze. "What do you say? You feel like coming out for a little while?"

He shrugged. "A little while would be okay, I guess."

Olivia looked skeptical. "It's kind of hard to work with so many people on one script."

"You can bounce ideas off us. Trust me. With all of us putting our heads together, we'll come up with the best ending ever."

She turned to Zeke. "Do you think if we write another song or two, you'll be able to put them to music?"

"I don't know," he said. "Depends how late it is."

"So let's get started," Max said. "Get your guitar and change."

Zeke's mother came back in the room. "Sorry to interrupt,"

she said. "I just wanted to know if you all want to stay for dinner."

"We're going to Trish's house," Zeke said, and walked off to his room.

A few minutes later, they were on the road, the girls in Trish's car, the guys in Zeke's, all of them heading off to a night shimmering with dramatic possibility.

CHAPTER SIXTEEN

Midnight. An open pizza box with an uneaten slice of pepperoni, the cheese hard and congealed, sits on the dining room table. A bottle of pinot noir, almost empty, stands uncorked next to a wine-stained glass. Olivia, in borrowed sweats and a T-shirt, types on the computer on the third floor, while Max, still wearing his chinos and button-down shirt from the funeral, makes coffee in the kitchen. Zeke is in the living room with his guitar, figuring out the music for the new song Olivia has finished, and Trish is asleep on the couch.

Max comes in, sees Trish sleeping, and smiles at Zeke. "How's it coming?"

He puts down his guitar, stands, and stretches. "Okay. How about you?"

"Just making some coffee for Olivia. You want some?"

Zeke shakes his head and yawns. "I'm probably gonna take off soon."

"Make sure you come up and say goodbye before you go."

Zeke nods, and Max heads back to the kitchen.

When Zeke hears Max go back upstairs, he begins to play something else and to sing very quietly. Trish wakes up and watches him through half-opened eyes before he notices her and stops playing.

"Don't stop." She sits up on the couch and rubs her eyes. "How long have I been sleeping?"

"About an hour."

She yawns. "Wow, I passed out." She blinks a few times, still not fully awake, and pulls her knees up to her chest and hugs them. "What's that you were playing just now?"

He looks down at his guitar. "Just something I wrote on the bus coming home yesterday," he says.

"Can I hear?"

He begins to fingerpick absently without looking up. "It's kind of personal."

She watches him until he looks up and meets her eyes, and she smiles at him. "Kind of feels like déjà vu, huh? Sitting here in the middle of the night working on a musical."

He nods and looks back down at his guitar.

"You know, that was the best part of last year for me."

He continues to look at his fingers as they dance across the strings.

Trish watches him for a moment, and then stands. "You want something from the kitchen?" she asks.

"No, thanks."

She walks out and comes back sipping from a can of Diet Coke. "Play something," she says, plopping down on the couch.

He starts to play his new song again, running through

the chords, and then finally beginning to sing. His eyes are downcast, his voice quiet, a haunted expression shrouding his face.

Got a call the other day
Jamie told me that you'd passed away
You'd started rehab back in May
I thought you'd be all right

Your life had spiraled in the last two years
Each time I saw you, you were shifting gears
But you seemed hopeful; you allayed my fears
Or I convinced myself

Never cared about convention
You made life your own invention
I know you had such good intentions
Devin

Always warm and always kind
Sense of humor, that creative mind
So much goodness left behind
Devin

All those stories that you told
The ones that left me feeling sad and cold
I wanted you to get a hold
You kept on giving in

I know that even when you lied
You were fighting; you really tried
What were you feeling deep inside?
Did you think you would live?

I look back and it is true
It was with you
When I would do
Those things I can't believe I did

But even so, those times we shared
Don't compare
To places where
You, in solitude, had slid

Got a call the other day
Jamie told me that you'd passed away
All those things I didn't say
I wish I'd said them now

He stops playing, but continues to stare down at his hand on the guitar. When at last he looks up, Trish's eyes are wet with tears.

"Wow," she says.

"I just talked to him a few days ago," he says quietly.

She comes to him, takes the guitar from his hands, leans down, and hugs him.

"I knew," he says, his voice choked. "I knew, and I didn't do anything."

"Shhh." She holds him tighter, and he buries his face in her shoulder and begins to sob.

She holds him even after he stops crying, until at last she feels him pulling away. He wipes his hand across his face. "I'm sorry about that," he says, avoiding her eyes.

"Don't be sorry," she says gently, and goes back to the couch.

He puts his guitar in the case and zips it up, trying to will his hands to stop shaking. "I should go say goodbye," he says.

"Come sit with me for a little."

"It's really late," he says, still not looking at her.

"Just for a minute."

He finishes zipping his guitar case, then sits on the couch and stares down at his legs.

"How are you doing?" Trish asks.

"I'm okay," he says. "I'm okay."

She takes his hand and squeezes it, and he squeezes her hand back.

"Take a minute for yourself," she says, getting up. "I'll go get them to come say goodbye."

He watches her go and then checks himself in the mirror and looks for his keys. When they come down, he is smiling, and he returns their hugs and promises to stay in touch. "I'm almost done with the new song," he tells Olivia. "I never realized there were so many ways to call someone drunk."

"There are a lot more than that if you Google it," Max says.

Olivia looks at Zeke and smiles. "Who knew he was such a good lyricist?"

"Get him to sing you his vampire song," Zeke says.

Olivia turns to Max and raises her eyebrows.

"Some other time," he says.

"I'm going to send you the rest of the play when I finish," she says. "Do you think you'll be up for writing any more music?"

"I'll do my best," he says.

They walk him outside to his car and stand in the driveway beneath a moon that is almost full, saying goodbye once more and waving as he drives off. Even after the car disappears from sight, they stand there, until Trish shivers and says she's ready to go to bed.

1:08 a.m. Trish has gone to sleep in her bedroom. Max and Olivia clean up from dinner and then plop down in the living room, Olivia on the couch, Max across from her in the recliner.

"I'm exhausted," she says.

"Should we drink some more coffee and try to get a little more done on the play?" His voice is tired and lacks conviction.

"I can barely keep my eyes open."

He yawns. "I know what you mean. We did a lot, though."

"We did," she says.

He looks at her and she looks at him, and he smiles at her in a way that says, "Isn't this nice?" and she smiles at him in a way that says, "It's very nice."

"Do you want a blanket?" he asks.

"Come sit with me," she says.

He gets up and moves next to her on the couch. They look at each other and smile some more.

"What are you thinking?" she asks.

He reaches over and brushes a strand of red hair out of her eye. "I wish I wasn't so tired."

She laughs and snuggles into him, and he puts his arm around her and gently strokes her hair.

"Mmm, that feels good." Her voice is far away.

They stay like that until he feels himself starting to doze off. He kisses the top of her head. "Come on," he whispers. "Let's find a bed."

She allows him to pull her up and lead her by the hand into the room they were in hours earlier. He takes off his shirt, and they lie down and begin to kiss, and there is something dream-like about it. They drift off in each other's arms, wake together and kiss some more. He feels her hand slide down and squeeze him through his chinos, and he unbuttons his pants and guides her hand beneath his boxers.

"Let me get these off," he whispers.

They both wriggle out of their clothes and intertwine their legs beneath the covers. His hands run down her back, and he embraces her more tightly.

"I don't have a condom," he whispers.

"Let's just go to sleep like this."

They kiss some more, and then she flips on her other side and nestles back into him.

He wraps his arms around her and buries his face in the back of her neck. "Good night," he whispers.

"Good night," she says, and clutches his hands.

CASTRATION CELEBRATION

Act 5, scene 1

(*The sounds of a large, raucous party come from offstage. Lola, Jesse, Carol, and Kitty stand outside.*)

KITTY: Are we really going in?

JESSE: Relax, will you? What do you think's gonna happen?

KITTY: I don't know, but I have a bad feeling about this.

LOLA: It's just a party.

CAROL: Yeah, at the house of the biggest homophobe in the whole school.

JESSE: That's what makes it so good.

KITTY: I just don't see how you're going to be able to videotape without someone noticing.

JESSE: The camera's tiny.

LOLA: Yeah, and everybody will probably be too drunk to notice, anyway.

KITTY: You really think nobody will notice you walking around with a video camera? No offense, Jesse, but you're not exactly the most discreet person I know.

JESSE (*holding out the camera*): You want to do it instead?

KITTY: No.

JESSE: Then shut the fuck up.

CAROL: Shhh. Look. (*Amber stumbles out with a cup of beer. She is wearing a very short skirt and is clearly drunk.*)

LOLA: I wouldn't mind having some footage of her.

KITTY: You pervert.

LOLA: What? You know she's hot.

CAROL: I'd do her.

JESSE (*to Lola*): Go try to kiss her. I'll film you.

LOLA: No way.

JESSE: Why not? She's obviously wasted. She's practically begging to be fucked.

LOLA: You think?

JESSE: Jesus, Lola, this is why you never get laid.

LOLA: Well, maybe I'll go say hi.

CAROL: Go for it.

(*Lola walks slowly toward Amber.*)

CAROL: Oh my God, you're filming this, right? (*The girls move off to the side and watch the scene unfold.*)

LOLA: Hey, Amber.

AMBER (*drunkenly, holding out her cup*): Lola Crest, Queen of the Lesbians. Are you as wasted as I am?

LOLA (*laughing*): I just got here.

AMBER: Well, get yourself a drink, girl, then come on back out and we'll have a toast.

LOLA (*looking around*): Are you here by yourself?

AMBER: I'm waiting for Dick to show up. (*starts to call out*) DICK? OH, DICK? WHERE ARE YOU? (*to Lola*) Have you seen Dick?

LOLA: Dick Conroy? He's not inside?

AMBER: He should be here, right? I mean, like, what the hell?

LOLA (*trying to hide her disappointment*): So you like Dick, huh?

(*Amber bursts out laughing, and Lola, realizing the double meaning, starts to laugh, too.*)

LOLA: That's not what I meant. I just didn't realize you and Dick were . . .

AMBER: What? Screwing? (*She laughs.*) Believe me, we're not.

LOLA: I didn't mean—

AMBER: It's okay. (*drinks from her beer*) So what's it like to be a dyke? Hey, that rhymed. Get it? Like, dyke?

LOLA (*laughing*): You're drunk.

AMBER (putting her arm around Lola's shoulder for
balance and starting to sing):

"I Don't Feel Any Pain"

(Amber)
I am blasted, blitzed, and bluttered
Gatted, goosed, and guttered
Loopy in my brain

I am minced and mashed and mangled
I am sizzled, smashed, and spangled
But I don't feel any pain

I am totaled, tanked, and tashered
Pickled, plowed, and plastered
Loopy in my brain

I am warped and wrecked and wasted
I am bladdered, bent, and basted
But I don't feel any pain

I am drunk
Just like a skunk
All my troubles fade away
And the stink of each passing day
Another drink

(*drains her cup and nearly falls over*)

> *I feel okay*

> (*Lola*)
>
> *I think you've had enough to drink*
> *Before you're puking in the sink*
> *Sit down in this chair*

(*They sit and Amber leans into Lola.*)

> *Lay your head upon my shoulder*
> *Take a rest until you're sober*
> *While I gently stroke your hair*

(*Lola begins to stroke Amber's hair.*)

(*softly, as if soothing a baby to sleep with a lullaby*)

> *Lay your head upon my shoulder*
> *Take a rest until you're sober*
> *While I gently stroke your hair*

AMBER: Mmm, that feels good.

LOLA: Your hair is so soft.

AMBER: I could fall asleep right here.

LOLA: Go ahead. (*Lola continues to stroke Amber's hair in a manner that becomes more and more sexual, and moves to her face, her shoulders, and her arms.*)

(*Dick walks onstage and watches the girls for a moment.*)

DICK: Hey, get a room, will you?

AMBER (*pulling away with a start*): Dick.

DICK (*smiling*): Wow, Amber, I had no idea.

AMBER (*defensively*): I was just resting. Right, Lola?

LOLA (*with obvious disappointment*): Right.

AMBER (*jumping up and throwing her arms around Dick*): I've been waiting for you all night.

LOLA (*hurt*): I need to get back to my friends. (*She walks off.*)

DICK (*disengaging himself*): Wow, you're really plastered, aren't you?

AMBER: Just a little. (*taking Dick's hand and pulling him away from the party*) Come on, I want to show you something.

DICK (*allowing himself to be pulled*): What?

(*Amber wraps her arms around Dick's neck and kisses him. He does not respond, and after a few seconds he pulls away.*)

DICK: Amber—

AMBER: No, it's okay. Jane said it was okay.

DICK (*pulling fully away*): What are you talking about?

AMBER: Jane. She said I could make out with you.

DICK (*dumbfounded*): Jane said that?

AMBER (*wrapping her arms around Dick again*): Uh-huh. (*She tries to kiss him again, and again he pulls away.*)

DICK: Wait, what exactly did she say?

AMBER: She said . . . (*Motioning for him to come close, she begins to whisper in his ear. The*

*implication is that she is whispering something
extremely lascivious, and Dick's eyes open wide as
he listens.*)

DICK (*pulling away and looking hard at Amber,
clearly trying to make up his mind about
something*): You're drunk, Amber. You don't know what
you're saying.

AMBER (*leaning hard against Dick*): I'm not drunk.
(*She tries to kiss him, and he gently pushes her
away.*)

DICK: You need to go home and sleep this off. Do you
want me to walk you home?

AMBER: No. I'm just gonna lie down here and take a
little rest. (*She lies on the ground and closes her
eyes.*)

DICK (*muttering to himself*): Jesus, why do I have to
deal with this? (*He looks around and sees Lola and
her friends watching the whole scene.*) Hey, can I
get some help over here?

(*The girls walk over.*)

DICK: Can you just watch her for a minute? I need to
run inside and find an empty room where she can

sleep this thing off. (*Dick runs offstage into the party.*)

JESSE (*pulling out her video camera*): So, Amber, do you have anything to say to our viewers today about what it's like to be a slut?

KITTY: Jesse, that is so mean.

CAROL: God, she's totally passed out.

LOLA: Maybe we should take her home.

JESSE: No way. I'm gonna follow them inside and get the whole thing on tape. I've heard about this kind of thing. A girl gets drunk at a party and a bunch of guys take turns raping her. Remember what happened at Duke a few years ago? With the lacrosse team?

LOLA: That didn't happen. She made the whole story up, remember?

JESSE: They just didn't have enough evidence. But this time I'll get the whole thing on tape and watch those bastards fry.

KITTY: You'd let them rape her just so you could tape it? That's like so wrong.

LOLA: No one's going to rape her.

(*Dick and Sluggo come running back onstage. The girls step back and Jesse hides her camera.*)

SLUGGO: Wow, she's totally passed out.

DICK: Come on, let's get her inside.

(*They lift her up.*)

SLUGGO (*smiling*): Too bad Biff's not here.

(*They exit.*)

JESSE: What did I tell you?

(*She pulls out her camera and rushes after them, the other girls following behind.*)

(*Curtain*)

CHAPTER SEVENTEEN

"Can we get copies of the tape?" Max asked, pausing beside the girl setting up the video camera.

It was the last night of the program, and people were beginning to stream into the auditorium for the end of the summer showcase, billed as a fabulous, fun-filled, final night of art, music, dance, and—of course—drama.

"We'll be sending them out next week to everyone who was here this summer," she said. "Are you performing tonight?"

"I'm doing part of her play," he said, turning and smiling at Olivia, who was standing beside him. "*Castration Celebration.*"

"Oh, yeah," she said with a grin. "I saw that in the program. Great title."

"Thanks," Olivia said, taking Max's hand and leading him to the aisle and down toward the seats in the front.

There were fifteen acts in total, and *Castration* was second to last. A week earlier, the students in Maxine's playwriting class had voted on two plays—Olivia's and Clarissa's—to represent the work of their class over the summer. Bruce had protested, of course, claiming it blatantly sexist not to include at least one male voice, but Maxine had silenced him by saying that to select a male play over a clearly superior female one would be a glaring example of affirmative action. Was that really what he wanted?

It had not been easy for Olivia to decide which scene to stage. What she really wanted was something that Max, Mimi, and Callie could perform on their own, without her having to find other students from the acting classes. And then there was the issue that so much of what she had written seemed too inappropriate to stage in such a public venue. She had sent her final scene off to Zeke to score, and when he had returned it the following day with music that absolutely rocked, she had decided that maybe this was the one to do. There was nothing overly obscene in the scene, and there were three main parts—one male and two female—with only a tiny fourth part that would be easy to fill.

"I wish Zeke was here to play the music," Olivia said.

"I've been trying all week to convince him." Over e-mail, Max had been waging his campaign—arguing that Zeke needed to get away from the scene back home, proposing that Zeke just show up and surprise everyone, guaranteeing Zeke a night of pleasure and debauchery—but to no avail. Zeke would be going to his father's the week before school started. That was all he could handle.

"You know Trish has been talking to him almost every day," Olivia said.

Max shook his head in disappointment. "I wish he had asked her out this summer."

"I don't know," Olivia said. "I mean, I know Trish likes him, but I'm not sure I can see them together. He doesn't really seem like the dating type."

"You weren't the dating type, either," Max joked.

"I'm still not. Haven't you figured out yet that I'm just using you for the sex?"

"We haven't even had sex," Max said.

Olivia feigned surprise. "We haven't? Are you sure? I must have mixed you up with one of those other guys I've been sleeping with. It's hard to keep you all straight."

"You keep me plenty hard and straight," Max said, leaning over and kissing her.

"Hey, get a room," Mimi called out as she and Callie came down the aisle and found seats in the row behind.

"Just practicing for our scene tonight," Max said. Mimi would be playing Jane opposite Max's Dick, and the action called for a considerable amount of lip locking. "I don't want you still thinking I kiss like a dead fish."

"Just don't get carried away up there," Olivia said, though in truth she was more concerned that the chemistry between the two actors be believable. That was why, in fact, she had cast Mimi in Jane's role instead of as the more obvious Amber. For that part, which required only talk and a quick kiss on the cheek, Callie had volunteered.

"Where's Trish?" Max asked.

"She was on the phone with Zeke again," Mimi said. "She said she'd meet us here."

The front of the auditorium was quickly filling up, and the lights began to dim and brighten, signaling the show was about to start. As everybody settled into seats, the MC, a short, pudgy boy wearing a knockoff tuxedo and flip-flops, walked onstage to thunderous applause.

"He's in my acting class," Max whispered to Olivia. "He's pretty funny."

"Hello, everyone," he said, waving to the audience. "My name is Brian, and it's been seventeen hours since I've had a drink."

Laughter rippled through the auditorium.

"Seriously," Brian continued. "How many of you are drunk right now?"

More laughter, and a few boys raised their hands.

"How many of you wish you were drunk?"

More laughter as Brian raised his own hand high.

"You know who's probably really drunk right now?" He paused dramatically, waiting to see if anyone would answer.

"The teachers," someone yelled out.

"Ding, ding, ding. Give that boy a cookie," Brian said. He looked over to the side section where most of the grown-ups were sitting and addressed them directly. "Admit it, guys. You all put a few back before coming here tonight, didn't you?"

The teachers chuckled appreciatively, and Brian launched into a few hilarious impersonations of select faculty members, before introducing the evening's first act.

Across the board, the performers were talented, and by the time act five ended, people were so swept up in the night's entertainment that nobody noticed two people—one with a guitar—slip into the auditorium and find seats in an empty row halfway down and off to the side. In fact, it was not until two more acts had finished that Olivia, turning in her seat to see if she could spot Trish, saw them, and her face broke into an enormous smile. She yanked Max's shirt, and when he turned, his face lit up, too. As the applause for the act died down, Max and the three girls hurried back to where Trish and Zeke were sitting and offered exclamations of surprise and delight.

"You have your guitar," Max whispered as the next performers took the stage. "Are you going to play with us?"

"I'd like to," Zeke said. "I was afraid I missed it."

"No, we've still got a while before we go on."

Act twelve was a long slideshow put together by the students in the art classes to highlight the work they had done over the summer. Act thirteen was an interpretive dance to the music of Beethoven and Britney Spears.

Backstage, Olivia huddled with the actors and then said a few words to Brian, who would be introducing the act. Max turned and looked at Zeke. He was sitting on a stool nearby, tuning his guitar. He strummed a few chords, and then looked up and locked eyes with Max. They both smiled.

"You ready?" Max asked.

Zeke nodded. "Let's do it."

The dance ended, and as applause echoed through the auditorium, Brian pirouetted onto the stage, arms flailing, and then looked up in mock embarrassment, as if he hadn't realized that anybody was watching him. "Our next act," he said, clearing his throat, "is a scene from Olivia Sands's musical *Castration*

Celebration. I'm not going to make any jokes about the title, because, frankly, I'm a little bit terrified right now."

Olivia walked out, smiling, and took the microphone. "First of all, nobody actually gets castrated, so you don't have to worry about that."

The audience laughed appreciatively, and she waited for the noise to die down.

"This is the final scene in the play," she said. "A quick summary of what's happened so far is . . ." She quickly recapped the key points in the plot, finishing at the party with a passed-out Amber being carried inside. "This last scene takes place the day after the party and opens with Jane and Amber sitting outside Jane's house, trying to piece together the events of the previous night."

CASTRATION CELEBRATION

Act 5, scene 2

(*The next day. Outside Jane's house. Jane and Amber sit on the stoop. Amber is wearing the same clothes she was wearing the night before. Her hair is disheveled, and she looks like she has been hit over the head with a sledgehammer.*)

JANE: You really don't remember anything?

AMBER (*shaking her head*): I was so drunk. I just passed out somewhere.

JANE: I can't believe you slept through the whole thing.

AMBER: So what happened?

JANE: I wasn't there, but Dick said that right after you passed out, Biff showed up really drunk and started screaming something about Sluggo wanting to rape him.

AMBER: What? That's crazy.

JANE: Apparently he was totally out of control, and when people tried to calm him down he started smashing things.

AMBER: Jesus, he's a total psycho.

JANE: You made out with him.

AMBER: Don't remind me.

JANE: So anyway, while Biff's going crazy, Doug Acker looks up and sees Jesse Dane filming the whole thing on a video camera and tries to grab it from her. Jesse screams, and Carol Shea jumps on Doug's back. Then Jesse pulls out a can of pepper spray and sprays Doug in the face.

AMBER: Holy shit.

JANE: He was screaming and clutching his eyes, and someone must have called 911 because three minutes later the police show up with an ambulance.

AMBER: I can't believe I slept through all this.

JANE: You were in a room upstairs with the door closed. After the cops cleared out the house, Dick called me on my cell and we snuck back in and got you.

AMBER: Are you serious? What time was this?

JANE: A little after midnight, I guess. My parents were asleep, so I had to sneak into their room to get the car keys. When I got there, Dick met me out front, but the door was locked so we couldn't get in. But Biff had smashed a couple of windows so we were able to clear away the glass and crawl through.

AMBER: You crawled through a broken window?

JANE: Yeah, it was pretty exciting. When we carried you downstairs, you opened your eyes a few times and mumbled some things that were totally incomprehensible. It was like three in the morning by the time we got you back to my house.

AMBER: Jesus. I must have been totally wasted.

JANE: You were in pretty bad shape.

AMBER: I'm sorry, Jane. I guess I totally screwed up the whole plan.

JANE (*smiling*): It's okay. In a funny way I think things might have worked out better this way.

AMBER: What do you mean?

JANE: You know, sneaking into houses with someone in the middle of the night can be quite a bonding experience.

AMBER: So you guys are back together?

JANE (*smiling*): Maybe.

AMBER: Maybe? What does that mean?

(*Jane smiles coyly.*)

AMBER: Hold on. Didn't you say that Dick called you at midnight?

JANE: Uh-huh.

AMBER: And you said that you didn't get me back here until three in the morning.

JANE (*smiling*): Something like that.

AMBER: Oh my God, did you guys have sex in front of me while I was passed out?

JANE: No. (*pause*) Not in front of you.

AMBER: Oh my God. You slut.

JANE: Well, how often do you get to sneak into a strange empty house in the middle of the night?

AMBER: That's unbelievable.

JANE: That's not all.

AMBER: Please tell me you didn't drag me into some perverse threesome.

JANE (*holds up a video camera*): Remember Jesse's video camera?

AMBER (*incredulously*): You filmed yourselves having sex?

JANE: You want to see?

AMBER: YUCK! NO!

JANE: Come on. (*hands her the camera*) Just press play.

AMBER: I don't want to see you and Dick having sex.

JANE: Trust me. You'll enjoy this.

AMBER: Are you serious?

JANE: I promise.

(*Amber takes the camera tentatively, looks into the viewer, and presses play. From offstage, we hear Dick's voice.*)

DICK: Is the camera on? Okay, here goes. I, Dick Conroy, being of sound mind and body, do hereby swear that I will always be loyal and faithful to my girlfriend, Jane Stanton. Furthermore, I swear that I will never make up stories about dying relatives so that I can sneak off with my friends to pick up skanky women in sleazy bars, nor will I act in any other way that might put undue stress on our relationship. If, at any time, I violate the terms of this agreement, I hereby agree to be tied up and locked in a room for a period of no less than one hour with Jesse Danes and a large, sharp knife of her choosing.

AMBER (*looking up*): I can't believe you got him to say this on tape.

JANE: When a guy is desperate enough, he'll promise anything.

AMBER: You wouldn't seriously hold him to this, though, would you?

JANE: If he cheats on me? You bet I would.

AMBER: Are you serious?

JANE: It's like you said. The penis has a mind of its own and can't be trusted to do the right thing. But if we instill enough fear into that penis, if we make that penis understand that its survival depends on keeping itself in check, then we can train it to act the way we want it to.

AMBER: Just don't scare it too much, or it will never want to come out and play.

JANE (*laughing*): Yeah, right.

(*Sam walks onstage in a baseball uniform with a baseball glove.*)

JANE: Good luck at your game, Sam.

SAM: Thanks. (*glances at Amber*) Bye, Amber.

AMBER: Wait. C'mere for a second. (*She gestures for Sam to come close, and then straightens his hat.*) Perfect.

SAM (*embarrassed, but extremely pleased*): Thanks.

(*Amber gives Sam a kiss on the cheek, and Sam blushes deeply.*)

AMBER: That's for good luck.

SAM (*hurrying off*): Bye.

JANE: He'll never wash that cheek again.

AMBER: I hope he hits a home run.

JANE: Let's just keep him on first base for now.

AMBER: You know, I think I'm going to give myself a nice long break from boys for a while. But when Sam turns eighteen, all bets are off.

(*The girls laugh. Dick walks onstage.*)

DICK: Good morning, ladies. (*He leans down and gives Jane a kiss.*)

JANE: I was just showing Amber the tape we made last night.

AMBER: You better behave yourself.

DICK: I know. What the hell was I thinking? (*He sits.*)

JANE (*wrapping her arms around Dick*): You were thinking how lucky you were to be getting another chance with the girl of your dreams.

DICK (*smiling*): Oh, yeah, now I remember. (*He kisses her.*)

AMBER: Well, I think I'll head home before I throw up all over both of you. (*She gets up and smiles at Dick.*) Thanks for rescuing me last night.

DICK: No problem. It was actually really fun.

AMBER: So I've heard. (*She exits.*)

DICK: You told her?

JANE: She guessed.

DICK: What did she say?

JANE: I think she called me a slut.

DICK (*laughing*): She should talk.

JANE: Hey. That's my best friend you're insulting.

DICK: Sorry.

JANE: Besides, she's sworn off boys until after she
graduates.

DICK: No way.

JANE: That's what she says.

DICK (*running his hand through her hair*): Well,
don't you go getting any ideas.

(*They kiss. Dick looks up with a glint in his eye.*)

DICK (*as Benedick*): Soft and fair, friar. Which is
Beatrice?

JANE (*catching on immediately, as Beatrice*): I
answer to that name. What is your will?

DICK (*as Benedick*): Do not you love me?

JANE (*as Beatrice*): Why, no; no more than reason.

DICK (*as Benedick*): Why, then, your uncle and the prince and Claudio have been deceived; for they swore you did.

JANE (*as Beatrice*): Do not you love me?

DICK (*as Benedick*): Troth, no; no more than reason.

JANE (*as Beatrice*): Why, then, my cousin, Margaret, and Ursula, are much deceiv'd; for they did swear you did.

DICK (*as Benedick*): They swore that you were almost sick for me.

JANE (*as Beatrice*): They swore that you were well-nigh dead for me.

DICK (*as Benedick*): Come, I will have thee; but, by this light, I take thee for pity.

JANE (*as Beatrice*): I would not deny you; but, by this good day, I yield upon great persuasion, and partly to save your life, for I was told you were in a consumption.

DICK (*as Benedick*): Peace! I will stop your mouth.

(*He kisses her. Music starts to play. They jump up and begin to sing.*)

"Let's Do a Little Shakespeare"

(*Dick*)

Before I met you, Beatrice
I was drifting all amiss
No idea where to steer
And then I found some Shakespeare

Yeah, I was ready to explode
All I wanted was to hit the road
Now I'm happy just to be right here
Let's do a little Shakespeare

(*Jane*)

Before I met you, Benedick,
Guys like you just made me sick
That day in class, I hold it dear
We did a little Shakespeare

Yeah, I remember how we clicked
I loved your quick wit, Benedick
You whispered sweet words in my ear
We did a little Shakespeare

(Dick)

We had a good thing, Beatrice
But I was thoughtless and remiss
When I lost you, I was filled with fear
Would we do more Shakespeare?

(Jane)

Benedick, you nearly blew it
If it looks good, you can't just screw it
I'm the only one, let's make it clear
Then we'll do more Shakespeare

(Dick)

Yeah, you're so sexy, Beatrice
Come on over, give me a kiss
Mmm, mmm, you taste better
than the finest beer
Come on, baby, shake my spear
Come on, baby, shake my spear

JANE (*laughing*): You're terrible.

DICK (*putting his arm around Jane and starting to walk offstage*): You know, Shakespeare actually wrote pornography in his spare time.

JANE (*playing along*): Did he really?

DICK: Little-known fact. He wrote a bawdy novel for Queen Elizabeth called *The Deflowering of the Virgin Queen*.

JANE: The things the history books leave out.

DICK: Tell me about it.

(*Curtain*)

CHAPTER EIGHTEEN

Max and Olivia held hands as they walked with their friends through the courtyard after the show. It was a warm night, but the air felt light and clean and crisp. Curfew had been extended an hour, so groups of students were everywhere—sitting on the stairs, standing around the statue of Nathan Hale, spreading blankets on the ground, popping in and out of dorms. Max felt torn between his desire to spend this last night hanging out and reminiscing with his friends—especially Zeke—and his awareness that it was also the last chance he would have to be alone with Olivia for a very long time. Tomorrow morning he would be leaving early, and by the afternoon he would be home in New Orleans, halfway across the country.

Olivia was feeling flushed and happy from the rousing ovation the play had received. Seeing Max up there, watching him bring Dick to life so brilliantly, she had wanted to throw herself on him and make out the moment he came offstage. She had restrained herself, of course, and she was restraining herself now, but soon, when they were alone, she was planning to body-slam him, the way he had body-slammed her the day they met.

"I can't believe this is really the last night," Mimi said.

Trish laced her arm through Zeke's. "We should do something wild and crazy."

"We could all get naked and streak around campus," Max suggested.

"I'll give you twenty dollars if you do it," Zeke said.

"Twenty dollars? No way."

"How much then?" Trish asked.

"To run all the way around the courtyard naked, with everyone out?" He thought about it for a moment. "A hundred from each of you, and I'd consider it."

"I'm not going to pay to see you naked," Callie said.

"That's too much," Mimi agreed.

"Then forget the money," Max said. "I'll do it if one of you does it with me."

They all looked at each other, hoping someone else would volunteer, but of course nobody did, much to Max's secret relief.

"We should get drunk," Trish said.

"Does anyone have alcohol?" Max asked.

Nobody did.

"I've got a joint we could smoke," Zeke said.

"You brought it with you?" Max asked.

"I've got to spend the next week with my dad and stepmom in fucking rural Virginia. You think I'd go empty-handed?"

"I'd smoke some," Callie said.

Max looked at Olivia, trying to gauge her reaction. "Not for me," she said, "but go ahead if you want to."

"I've never done it before," Trish said. She looked up at Zeke. "Will you show me how?"

Mimi shook her head. "I can't believe you guys. It's so bad for you."

"No worse than drinking," Callie said. "Spark it up."

"You're going to smoke here?" Mimi look horrified. "People can see. They can smell. We're right near the gate to the street."

"Nobody's looking," Zeke said, pulling out the joint. "Just face away and act normal."

"I'm going back to the dorm," Mimi said.

"I'll go with you," Olivia said.

"Wait," Max said. "We can all go back."

"Don't worry about it," Olivia said. "Just come find us when you're finished breaking the law."

Max looked at her. "Are you sure?"

"It's fine," she said, kissing him on the cheek. "It's kind of hot dating a criminal."

"Maybe I'll go with you guys," Trish said. "Will you come find me when you're done?" she asked Zeke.

"Sure," he said. "We'll be there in a few minutes."

Zeke lit the joint and passed it to Callie. She took a small hit, and then a second one when the joint came back to her. "That's it for me," she said, handing it to Max. "I'm going to head back to the room and see if we have any cookies."

"Save some for us," Max called after her.

"Cool chick," Zeke said.

Max nodded, took a long drag, exhaled, and smiled at Zeke. "It's good to see you, man."

"Good to be here," Zeke said, accepting the joint and taking a huge hit.

Max looked around the courtyard. "Yale Fucking University," he said. "You remember getting high the first night we were here?"

Zeke smiled in reminiscence. "I remember your dad calling when you were totally wasted."

"Unbelievable," Max said, shaking his head. "He did that like every time I got high this summer."

"You think he'll call now?"

"Oh, shit." Max took his cell phone out of his pocket and turned it off. He had already talked to his father earlier in the day, but there was no reason to take any chances. And if he was going to be with Olivia soon, he certainly did not want any interruptions.

"So what about you and Trish?" he asked, taking the joint. "You going to get together with her tonight?"

Zeke blushed slightly. "I don't know. I'm thinking about it."

"You totally should."

"What are we going to do about sleeping arrangements?" Zeke asked.

Max considered this. "It could work if Mimi will move into Callie's room. Then I could stay in Olivia's room, and you and Trish could have ours."

"That works," Zeke said.

Max took another hit off the joint and thought about Olivia and the night that lay ahead of them. Everything had fallen into place. Zeke was here, and the performance had rocked, and they were getting good and high, and soon they would be heading in to the girls, who were waiting. He handed Zeke the joint. "We're both getting laid tonight, right?"

Zeke took a hit, smiled, and began to thrust his hips back and forth. "Bang, bang, bang, bang, bang."

It was at this moment that a New Haven policeman, passing by the campus gate on High Street, looked in and saw them.

EPILOGUE

To: olivia123@comcast.com
From: maxmania@gmail.com
Subject: I'm an idiot

Dear Olivia,

I, Max Diamand, being of (questionably) sound mind and body, do hereby swear that I will never again choose the cheap thrill of getting high over the much deeper and more pleasurable experience of spending time with my girlfriend, Olivia Sands. Furthermore, I swear that I will never engage in any behavior that will lead to arrest and incarceration, and that if, by chance, I am arrested and incarcerated, I will remain loyal

and faithful to the extent that it is in
my power to do so.

There. Now it's in writing.

I don't know if my dad is going to let
me out of his sight again until I go
away to college, but I'll sneak off when
he's sleeping if I have to, fly to
Hartford, and climb in your window. One
way or another, I'll figure out a way to
see you again, because we still have
some unfinished business to attend to.
Criminally yours,
Max

To: maxmania@gmail.com
From: olivia123@comcast.com
Subject: Re: I'm an idiot

Dear Max,
You must know from the play that the idea
of you sneaking into my house in the
middle of the night is a real turn-on.
Just tell me what night you'll be here,
and I'll leave the back door unlocked.
Olivia/Jane/Beatrice

To: olivia123@comcast.com
From: maxmania@gmail.com
Subject: Re: I'm an idiot

Three girls for the price of one. I like it.

To: olivia123@comcast.com, maxmania@gmail.com, mimibear@yahoo.com, calliegirl@aol.com
Cc: zekeusfreakus@earthlink.net
From: pixystixeater@yahoo.com
Subject: reunion

Hi, everyone,

Great news. My parents said I could invite all of you to stay at our house during Columbus Day weekend. I know we just came home three days ago, but I wanted to let you know as soon as possible before you make any other plans. I hope you all can come. I miss you already.

Love,

Trish

P.S. No drugs allowed!

To: pixystixeater@yahoo.com,
maxmania@gmail.com, mimibear@yahoo.com,
calliegirl@aol.com
Cc: zekeusfreakus@earthlink.net
From: olivia123@comcast.com
Subject: Re: reunion
Attachments: castrationfinalscene.doc

Hey, guys,
Count me in for Columbus Day weekend.
Maybe we can work on college
applications together. Trish, are you
still planning to apply to Yale early
action? How funny would it be if you end
up back in our dorm?

I decided the musical needed one more
scene. If anybody ever turns this thing
into a movie, this would be the part to
roll with the final credits. Enjoy.
Olivia

CASTRATION CELEBRATION
Act 5, scene 3

(*In a holding cell. Sluggo and Biff sit next to
each other on a bench, staring straight ahead.
Neither one talks for several seconds. When they
begin to speak, they do not look at each other.*)

SLUGGO: How do you feel?

BIFF: Like shit. (*pause*) You?

SLUGGO: I've been better.

(*They sit for a while in silence, and then both begin to speak at once.*)

SLUGGO and BIFF: Listen—

(*They look at each other and smile.*)

SLUGGO: Go ahead.

BIFF: No, you first.

SLUGGO: Look, I'm sorry for . . . you know, that shit I pulled. I don't know what came over me.

BIFF: Yeah, well, I'm sorry for fucking up your party and breaking your parents' windows and shit.

SLUGGO: It's okay.

(*They sit in silence for a while.*)

BIFF: So what's the deal? You like to swing both ways or something?

SLUGGO (*shaking his head*): I don't know. It's
confusing.

BIFF: What does that mean?

SLUGGO: I don't know. It just is.

(*They continue to sit in silence.*)

SLUGGO: Can you believe this shit? My fucking
parents won't even cut their trip short to get me
out of jail.

BIFF: My parents aren't even away, and they still
won't come.

SLUGGO: Assholes.

BIFF: Tell me about it.

(*They continue to sit in silence.*)

BIFF: So what's it like?

SLUGGO: What?

BIFF: You know. Doing it with another guy.

SLUGGO: I don't know. I only did it once.

BIFF: What was it like?

SLUGGO: Why are you so interested?

BIFF: I'm not.

(*They continue to sit in silence.*)

SLUGGO: It hurt a little. But in a good way.

BIFF: That's nasty, man.

SLUGGO: Fuck you. You're the one who asked.

BIFF: You didn't have to be so graphic.

(*They continue to sit in silence.*)

BIFF: I'd fuck a sheep before I'd fuck another guy.

SLUGGO: I know you would, Biff. I know you would.

(*Curtain*)

THANKS TO:

My agent, Marcia Wernick, and my editor, Jim Thomas,
for continuing to advise, guide, support, and edit me
with such warmth and intelligence

My eighth-grade students at Salk, past and present,
for all the great conversations in class, even
the ones I wasn't supposed to hear

Adam, Allie, Alyssa, and Katy, for sharing details
about life in a summer program at Yale

Mom, Dad, and Ben, for providing so much raw material
for the last book, and for not changing the family name
when you heard the title of this one

Marvin and Elie, for embracing the fact that the person who
wrote this book is sharing a bed with your daughter

Hilary, for giving me that line

Leilani and Cecily, for inspiring my silly side

And especially Kira, for making it all possible

JAKE WIZNER grew up in a dormitory at Yale, and some of his fondest childhood memories took place on the Old Campus, where this story is based. These days he lives in New York City with his wife and two young daughters and spends his time writing, teaching, and going to the playground.

Jake's first book, *Spanking Shakespeare,* was an ALA-YALSA Best Book for Young Adults. Learn more about Jake by visiting his Web site at www.jakewizner.com.